BEYOND
PLAIN SIGHT

DOMINIC BLYE

BEYOND
PLAIN SIGHT

To my mother, whose strength and love shaped me and gave me the courage to grow. Your belief in me, even when I doubted myself, is my guiding light.

To Raheem and Gabby, my joy and inspiration — may this book remind you that with heart, love, and perseverance, anything is possible. This work exists because of you all, and for the legacy of love you bring to my life

Acknowledgements

First and foremost, I want to thank **God**—the Author of my faith. Every breath, every page, and every word that has found its way into this story exists because of His grace. Without Him, there would be no me. It is His power that continues to lift me when I feel weak, His wisdom that guides me when I cannot see the road ahead, and His love that reminds me that I am never walking alone.

Writing this story has not been easy. There have been days when the words refused to come, when the weight of doubt pressed so heavily on my heart that I questioned whether I was meant to finish at all. I wrestled with thoughts of giving up, wondering if anything I wrote could ever hold meaning or truth. Yet, every time I reached that breaking point, His gentle whisper reminded me why I began—to create something that reflects His goodness, even through my own imperfections.

It was often in the silence of the deepest night that I felt His presence most intensely. He was there, not to write the words for me, but to steady my hand and renew my weary mind. The true victory of this book is not in its completion, but in the unwavering belief that sustained me through the process.

This journey has been one of faith as much as creativity—proof that when you trust God's timing and surrender your fears, He can transform even your weakest moments into something purposeful. Every scene born out of frustration, every late night spent searching for the right words, has become a testimony of perseverance and grace. The struggles were never in vain; they were shaping both the story and the storyteller.

Every character, every moment of despair and triumph within these pages, is a reflection of His mercy and the strength He has placed within me. What once felt like a burden became a blessing, and what felt meaningless found purpose in His plan. For that, I am eternally grateful.

The Foundation

My family is the foundation of my being and the heart that beats behind everything I do—you are my beginning, my home, and my constant reminder of love in its purest form. Each of you has added something unique: laughter, encouragement, love, and a reminder that life is richer when shared. You've proven that a family's bond isn't just built on blood—it's built on time, trust, and shared dreams. Like the saying goes, "It takes a village," and I am endlessly thankful for mine. You are that village—my tribe—and I wouldn't be who I am without you.

I owe so much to my mother, **Sandra**—my greatest supporter, my truest friend, and the heartbeat of my life. Your strength, compassion, and endless encouragement have carried me through every trial and triumph. You have been there through my storms, praying for me when I couldn't find the words, believing for me when I had lost sight of my own strength, and cheering for me when I needed to believe again. Your love has been the steady hand on my shoulder, reminding me that no dream is too far, no fall too deep, and no failure too final. You've taught me that greatness isn't found in perfection, but in persistence—in rising every time life asks if you still believe. You are my home, my peace, and my reminder that love can hold even the heaviest burdens. I love you more than words could ever express. You've always been my heart, my guide, and my grounding light.

This book is, in many ways, a reflection of **you**. Every word, every chapter, and every moment of hope between the lines carries the imprint of your love and the lessons you've poured into me. It is something tangible—a lasting mark that I hope will echo long after the final page is turned. You taught me the meaning of sacrificial love, and it is that lesson that breathes life into the pages of this book. I pray I have made you proud, because any good found within these pages began with the good you instilled in me.

This story was written from a place of love, faith, and reflection. My immediate family—**Raheem and Gabby**—you are my greatest blessings.

You are the living proof that love multiplies, that purpose grows with each new heartbeat, and that the legacy we build is not written in ink, but in the lives we touch. You are my light, my grounding force, and the dearest audience for all the stories I've yet to tell. Knowing I have your love waiting for me at the end of every chapter was my greatest motivation. Your laughter reminded me why I create, your patience gave me the grace to finish, and your belief in me made every long night worth it. You are the precious, living poetry of my life, far more beautiful and complex than any story I could ever invent.

Every time I see your faces, I'm reminded why I keep pushing, why I keep believing, and why love always wins in the end. This book is a piece of me—but more importantly, it's a piece of us. It's something I pray you'll hold onto as you grow into the people, I know you're meant to be: strong, compassionate, and faithful. Let it remind you that even when life feels uncertain, you come from love—and that love endures all things. You are my daily inspiration, my safe harbor, and the living legacy I hope to leave in motion. Thank you for simply existing and giving my world the profound meaning that fueled this work from start to finish. This journey, though often marked by doubt and weariness, has been one of discovery—of who I am, who I love, and who I strive to become. Writing this book has been both a battle and a blessing, a mirror and a prayer. And in every line, I see the faces of those who made it possible.

And to **Kelly**—thank you for allowing me to share the beauty of family with the world. Without you, I would never have known the depth of what it means to be a father. You've given me the eyes to see life through a lens of gratitude and grace. You've taught me that love is not just something we feel—it's something we *live*, every single day, in the quiet sacrifices, the laughter shared, and the unwavering belief that tomorrow can always be better than today.

My First Teachers

My brothers, **Christopher and William**, you are my lifelong mirrors. Am I my brother's keeper? Always. You've both been there through thick and thin, reminding me of who I am when the world tried to tell me otherwise. You've taught me the power of loyalty, laughter, and brotherhood. Life's journey would have been far heavier without your support and your faith in me. I thank you for walking beside me every step of the way. From childhood adventures to adult challenges, your presence has been the consistent, unshakeable backdrop to my life, providing a strength that needed no words.

I also want to recognize my aunts **Cynthia and Dorothy, and my uncle James Thomas**. Each of you has left an imprint on my life that cannot be measured. You've shown me the importance of faith, patience, and seeing the world through different lenses. You've celebrated my wins, comforted me in my losses, and taught me that family isn't just who you're born to— it's who you grow with. Your collective wisdom acted as a compass, guiding me during moments of confusion and proving that there are many ways to walk a path of purpose.

My grandmother **Teresa** is the soul of our family—you have been a well of wisdom and grace. Your quiet strength has inspired generations, and your love has been the glue that keeps us bound together. You are the keeper of our history and the tender reminder of where we came from. And to the loving spirit of my grandfather **Thomas**, though you may no longer walk this earth, your presence is felt in everything I do. Your resilience, discipline, and quiet dignity live on in me. Every time I rise after falling, I feel you there—pushing me forward, whispering that I was made for more. The lessons of character and hard work you left behind are the bedrock upon which my creative life is built.

Friends and Supporters

I am deeply grateful for my extended family and friends, whose presence in my life continues to remind me of the simple, lasting power of joy, laughter, and loyalty. Each of you has added something special to my story—memories that still make me smile, lessons that helped me grow, and moments that reminded me how much richer life becomes when shared with others. You've been there through every high and low, through late-night talks and quiet moments of understanding, and I carry the weight of that love with deep appreciation.

To my best friend, **Nigel**—you've been more than a friend; you've been my brother. From the days when our biggest worries were just dreams too big for our age, to the nights when life felt heavy and uncertain, you've stood by me with a loyalty that few ever find. You've seen me at my best and at my worst, and through it all, you never stopped believing in me. Your faith in who I am, even when I struggled to see it myself, has been one of the greatest gifts of my life.

Our bond is something I do not take for granted. It's built on years of shared laughter, late-night conversations, hard truths, and mutual respect. You've taught me that friendship isn't just about being there when it's easy—it's about showing up when it's hard, when words fall short, and when silence says enough. That kind of loyalty is rare, and I want you to know that you have my greatest support, always.

To all my friends who have walked beside me, cheered me on, and reminded me to keep going—thank you. You've filled my life with warmth and belonging. This book, in many ways, is a reflection of the people who stood behind me when I doubted myself the most. The laughter we've shared, the memories we have built, and the loyalty we've kept—those are the things that make the struggles worthwhile. I am endlessly grateful for every one of you.

Thank you to **Logan, Marcus, Tony, Anthony, Zack, and Joe**. You poured countless conversations, inspiration, support, and motivation into me over the years. You've all helped shape my journey, directly or indirectly, and left a lasting impact that I'll always carry forward. Sometimes it only takes a few words of encouragement to light a fire—and you've each done that for me in your own way.

For everyone who supported this project and believed in my vision— **Rick, Rose, LaShawn, Bartuo,** and so many others—thank you. Every piece of advice, every edit, every late-night message of encouragement has meant more than I can express. You've helped turn what began as an idea into a finished work that carries my voice, my truth, and my heart. Thank you for seeing potential even when I was too deep in the process to see it myself. You reminded me that creation is not done alone—it's a collaboration of faith, love, and community.

My Creative and Production Village

To the team of talented professionals who helped me transform a manuscript into a finished book, my gratitude is immense. As a self-published author, this work would not exist without your dedication, expertise, and belief in my vision.

Katarina, thank you for capturing the heart and soul of this story and translating it into a cover that speaks volumes. And **Walt**, thank you for your skill in bringing structure and beauty to every page and turning the text into a truly professional read.

My **beta readers and advance reviewers**, you were my first, most critical audience. Your honesty and willingness to engage with the earliest drafts gave me the confidence and direction needed to cross the finish line. This collaborative effort proves that a writer is never truly alone in the creation process. Every one of you is a co-architect of this dream, and I thank you for treating my work with the care and excellence it deserved.

Lastly, to everyone reading this book, to every person who has supported, encouraged, and believed in this vision—thank you. You are part of this story now. Whether you offered a word of kindness, shared a moment of belief, or simply turned these pages with curiosity in your heart—know that you are appreciated. This journey has not been easy, but it has been worth every step because of the people who walked beside me, near or far. It is my sincere hope that the narrative within these pages resonates with your own life experiences and offers you a sense of encouragement or hope. Knowing that my words have found their way to you completes the cycle of creation.

From the bottom of my heart, thank you all—for your love, your patience, your faith, and your presence. You have made this book, this dream, and this moment possible. I carry your support with me always, and I look forward to the journey that lies ahead.

With endless love, gratitude, and humility.

Table of Contents

Chapter 1

The Never-Ending Chase

Nesting against the back wall of the modest room stood a tall oak bookshelf. Its smooth frame glowed in the lamplight, which was housed within a glass etched with delicate swirls. The oak wood looked as if it possessed ageless wisdom, but it was the carving upon its surface that drew attention: a lush jungle scene full of life. Monkeys sprang from gnarled vines that grew tightly around ancient trees. Birds with large wings and knowing eyes darted from the foliage as snakes basked in the underbrush. In the heart of the scene, hidden among the trees, a hunter stalked his prey: a lion crouched beneath a fern, unaware of the shotgun's barrel aimed squarely at it. Lurking above them, barely noticeable to the untrained eye, was a motionless leopard crouching on a twisted branch. With tense muscles and narrowed eyes, it waited to spring. The predator stalked the predator. The cycle of danger and irony was immortalized in wood forever. Near the top of the bookcase, burned shallowly but delicately into the grain, were the words: IGNORANCE IS BLISS. The letters glimmered in the light, their meaning echoing deeper than the eye could perceive.

Within the glass case were shelves with rows of accolades: awards from various press organizations, plaques bearing praiseworthy accomplishments, and certificates of excellence. Among them was the Global Shining Light Award for investigative journalism, which stood out from all honors. On the surrounding walls, photos in decorative frames told a calmer, more intimate tale. Candid moments of life were captured in vibrant locations: a couple holding hands on the cliffs of Santorini, laughing beneath cherry blossoms in Kyoto. They were smiling, continuously in motion, like the world they inhabited. Love was evident in each glance and gesture; all caught forever behind glass.

A moment of brief silence filled the small, dimly lit room. The stillness was almost sacred, disturbed only by the pulsing current of electricity running through the walls. This peace was temporary before movement swept through the space.

A subtle shift. And then...

There were quick, jolting movements in the living area, as if a spirit were moving through the space, ruffling documents and paperwork. With each crunching sound of crinkling paper, a document was taken from its place and then moved somewhere else.

Looking around the room, the exhaustion was clearly visible in the dark circles and tension on a man's face. "This was maddening. I should be asleep in my bed," Amore Reyes muttered, "But I must double-check everything for tomorrow's meeting. I have jumped through all these hurdles, and this will be another one. In the next few hours, I will have editors and "half-assed" people who don't know what's going on with my work, who will be critiquing and ridiculing all my information. No matter the cost, I must make sure this is right."

From the adjacent room emerged a man—tall, wiry, and clean-shaven. His salt-and-pepper hair fell like silk over his forehead. His frame, though lean, held a quiet strength, the kind built from years of running on adrenaline and instinct. He was shirtless, wearing a pair of well-fitted blue boxers. Looking disheveled, yet entirely in control. Bouncing from one location to another, he felt the urgency with each step. Perhaps it was his desire which overpowered his will, so exhaustion had no place in what was driving this reaction. Each movement spawned another movement.

"Why," he muttered to himself, "is that not correct? Regarding the source, you know that needs to be removed and an asterisk added."

Amidst the obscurity, in the small corner of the room, a pale golden light glowed from a single desk lamp in the back. On top of the small wooden office desk sat a thin computer monitor that hummed with life, its screen casting a soft, bluish glow that wandered throughout the room. The surface was barely visible beneath a tidal wave of manila folders, every one of them bulging with case files, redacted memos, printed emails, and handwritten notes. The desk was nearly buried beneath an avalanche of secrets. Pressed against the bottom of the desk was a solid black leather briefcase, well-worn. The pockets were overflowing with photographs and other documentation, a few of which were bursting the edges. Post-it notes stuck on a few sections read such things as: Follow up on source, do not trust, check facts, and a circled phrase: They're watching.

He dove into the chair in front of the monitor without hesitation, instinctively grasping for the briefcase beside him. His fingers flew with frantic speed, rummaging through folders and sorting papers as if answers were on the verge of slipping from his mind.

Stopping abruptly. His fingers had landed on a particular document. Pulling it out slowly and placing it on the desk. His black, deep, unflinching eyes were locked onto the screen as his hands began to move. Rapid keystrokes echoed in the room like gunfire, purposeful and unyielding. His bare, tensed back arched as he leaned forward, the muscles shifting beneath his skin with each movement. In his right hand, his pen drummed against the desk rhythmically, a symphony of clicks, taps, strokes, and the catch of a man too consumed to notice his own exhaustion.

Thoughts became words. Words became sentences. The screen filled with his truth.

The noise grew as each keystroke dropped with the weight of discovery until the noise spilled out into the hall, winding through walls like a ghost. "That's right, this will have to go on the government source for greater clarity," he grumbled to himself.

The cursor blinked at the end of a sentence he'd written and rewritten four different ways, but his eyes weren't focused on the screen anymore. He closed his eyes for a few moments to catch up with his thoughts and to remind himself why he was doing this story. Fixating back on the screen, a single name was the catalyst for this passion that was like both a threat and a promise—Gargon Maxwell, burning in his soul each time it reappeared

To the public, Gargon Maxwell was a man who could do no wrong. No matter what happened to him, he always stood tall. The scent of corruption emanated from him and his company NewTech, but it didn't matter because no one could see it. His name and corporation kept reappearing in some shape or form. It was a name soaked in red flags.

For months now, he'd fought tooth and nail with fact-checkers sending him in circles, sources disappearing, and legal teams hesitating. Each version of the story came back red-marked and gutted. But the facts he had—those that survived—remained unchanged, unshakable.

"Amore…" The gentle voice of a young woman stirred from the adjacent room, low, soft, and still weighed down by sleep. She turned over, stretching, extending her arm to the empty space beside her, half-snuggled in the warm creases of their bed. "Babe. You said you were going to get some water." She paused, her voice tinged with a drowsy frustration. "That was a few hours ago. Come back to bed... just for a little bit longer."

He didn't stop typing. Only his voice replied, low and persistent: "I'm nearly finished, Melanie," he whispered. She stirred. "You're being too noisy again. If you're going to work, at least let me sleep."

He glanced over his shoulder. Moonlight through the blinds stripped her naked shoulder, silhouetting her in silver. Her hand reached for the pillow where his head should have been. "I miss holding you at night," she whispered. "You're always gone somewhere, chasing the next headline."

He looked at the door, then at her. For a moment, he considered it—really considered it. Letting go of the article for an instant. Climbing into bed. Sleeping straight through the rest of the night with her. Feeling the stillness of her heartbeat on his chest. Letting the sun rise without resistance. God, it was tempting—the warmth, her flesh, the tug of a life he used to know how to live. He hovered in thought. Maybe five minutes. Maybe he'd slip back in, kiss the back of her shoulder, bury his face in her back, and let sleep take him. Yet his eyes flicked back to the laptop screen. With a slow, steady tone, he looked down at the keyboard. Then up at the door again. He wanted to—he really did—but when his eyes landed on the headline draft again, he was focused. Maxwell. He was close. Closer than he'd ever been. The headline throbbed like a heartbeat: ***Empire of Silence: The Hidden Crimes of Gargon Maxwell***.

This should be the last meeting. Only one more set of eyes for the final nod of approval. Then the dominoes could fall. This was months of work: dodging contradictions, resubmitting documents, defending every quote and claim to a gauntlet of editors and legal advisors. The uphill battle hadn't slowed him—it hardened his resolve. There were inconsistencies within the narratives of the story, yes, but also a haunting consistency in the buried truths. There was something here. But first, he turned back toward the bedroom door.

Amore exhaled, saved the file for the fifth time, and lingered. The allure of Melanie's warmth was immense, but the Gargon Maxwell story beckoned. Weighing what was before him, he decided: it was best that he leave immediately and proceed to the office. He rose from the desk, the slim computer monitor still on. He filled his backpack with the rhythm of ritual, grabbing his USB drives, folders, red-marked copies, scribbled notes, and a hard drive full of recordings. He moved like a thief, stealing his own time.

He would go over everything again with Greg, a close friend and Assignment Editor at The Inquisitor, before the meeting with Jim, the Editor-in-Chief. That was the final obstacle.

Amore glanced over his shoulder at the bedroom. He needed to get dressed without disturbing Melanie. Slowly making his way towards the room, he started reaching for his blue blazer but then, with a drastic change, his body relaxed in doubt. Starting to walk closer towards the foot of the bed, his knees began to feel weak and then he stood still. Finally, he climbed in—just for a minute.

Crawling under the sheets alongside her body, he automatic-ally wrapped his arms around her. She groaned, folding into him instinctively, smiling dreamily as she nestled her body into his. Their legs tangled. Behind him, Melanie shifted under the blankets. She muttered something incoherent, and then whispered, "Oh, you feel so good."

There was a brief moment of intimacy, and then it abruptly ended with Melanie painfully saying, "But you're not staying, are you? You were up pacing before you even got into bed. That meeting's already working itself out in your head." " You don't have to lie," she yawned. "I know your routine. It begins with you getting quiet and restless when your head is already somewhere else. You have been up for hours writing and rewriting your story." He didn't answer. Then hesitated. "I" "You may go," she said, playfully taunting. " Stop pretending you're not trying to sneak out again. I know you." "I need to get up anyway," she sighed. "I have to review some proposals later today," her eyes still closed. "You're cold. You never let yourself sleep."

"I will," he said softly. "Soon."

She nestled closer. "I need to review those pitch notes for Verity & Co. The new client we're working with in health tech messaging is a disaster. They're always trying to be clever when they just need to be clear," she said as she started to sit up in their bed.

He smirked, recognizing the firm tone she used with clients. She was a PR strategist at heart—clean, sharp, professional. She turned, facing him, her eyes open. "Go before I regret it. Your mind is already halfway out the door anyway." "I love you," he said to her. He kissed her forehead. She smiled, eyes closed. "You know me too well." "I do," she whispered. "Now go." She nudged him gently and he stood, running a reluctant hand over his back, picking up his clothes and beginning to get dressed. "My meeting with Jim at the office will not be easy," he muttered as he put on his shirt. "I'll call you after."

Chapter 2

The Price of the Truth

The Inquisitor newsroom was a ghost town when Amore arrived at 6:52 a.m. It was the calm before the storm. A few early-rising reporters were already at their cubicles, mug in hand, squinting at their screens, trying to get a head start on the chaos. Phones began to ring, and the air was thick with the scent of freshly brewed coffee. A janitor pushed a cart silently along the walls, which were covered with whiteboards, pinned-up notes, and half-erased timelines of past stories that had either blown up or died in committee.

Amore walked in like he belonged there but was always fighting to prove it.

A voice he knew called out from the other side of the bullpen. Greg was sitting at an adjacent desk with a steaming cup of coffee and a spread of printed pages—waiting.

"Jesus, you look like shit," Greg said, clapping his hands together.

Amore smirked. "Thanks for the warm welcome. This is an early morning for you; normally you are sleeping in somewhere."

Greg shrugged, grinning. "Yeah, well, someone had to make sure you didn't die on the finish line." Noticing the tired look on Amore's face, clear evidence he'd worked through the night, Greg said in a mischievous tone, "From the looks of things, you've been burning the candle at both ends again." Cup in hand, sipping the coffee religiously, he leaned towards Amore and offered to get him some. "It's going to be a long meeting," he said. "You need to be in better shape than you are now."

Amore laughed. "Didn't peg you for the rescue type. Besides, I am at my best in this state. You should know me by now. I thrive on these moments."

Greg shook his head with a sharp counter. "This isn't just a moment. This is make-or-break. If it doesn't go well in this meeting with Jim, then it's back to the drawing board."

"Normally I try to stay away from any assignment you are working on, but per your request, I am here enjoying the morning, not my bed," Greg replied, handing him a mug. "But I come for the friends who don't have the decency to ask for backup earlier."

With an anxious look, he added, "I haven't had the time to thoroughly review your completed notes and information. I know you brought me into this meeting, and I've only been briefed on small nuances of it. So, it's good we can come together beforehand and go through all the details."

"You've been working on this all night?" Greg asked, observing the dark circles under his eyes.

"Rewriting, mostly," Amore replied, setting down his bag and yawning. "Fact checkers flagged the senator quote again, despite my sending the source tape."

Greg waved it off. "They're scared. You're pulling threads no one wants pulled."

Greg chuckled, motioning to a side table. "C'mon, let's run through it."

They sat, Greg thumbing through the latest printout Amore handed him—annotated, dog-eared, stained by stress and caffeine.

"You're still chasing Maxwell," Greg muttered, flipping through the pages.

Amore didn't respond immediately. He surveyed the rising motion of the newsroom—the chatter, the clacking keys, the scent of newsprint and tension. "I am not chasing," Amore said. "I am documenting. This is the story. It is not about the money, or the contracts that vanished, or the private jets to nowhere. It is about power masquerading as invisible."

Greg exhaled through his nose. "What if this doesn't pan out? What if all you end up with is a headline and a cease and desist? And what if you go into the meeting with this and Jim kills it—again? He believes the whole thing's thin, risky. Says it's all theory wrapped in a righteous tone. He wants it dead on arrival."

"This story," he murmured, "is bigger than they know. Bigger than even we know."

"The truth will be told," Amore said, sitting upright, eyes shining. "No matter who hears it."

Greg looked at him for a long time, then sighed and began to sift through the papers on his desk. "Well then. Let's make some people upset."

Greg leaned back, watching him. There was admiration, but real concern too

"You've done good work before—significant stories have come to light. You've created ripples. But this?" He tapped the pile. "You're ruffling feathers. Creating enemies. You really want to keep pushing this?"

Amore didn't hesitate. "If I don't speak for us, who will? The voiceless don't have a voice—and the man I am gives them one. I am the speakerphone they scream through."

Greg's eyebrow rose. "Okay, okay—cut the egotistical bullshit monologue," he said, grinning. "You don't need to sell me on this. You need to sell Jim. And the people who will also be in that room." Greg continued reading the lead-in paragraph, then his eyebrow rose. He opened the folder, flipping through charts, screenshots, internal memoranda. " Is this what kept you out of Melanie's bed last night?"

A pause. Then Amore edged in. "I'm near, Greg. This is no story—it's the kind of thing that ruins legacies. Or builds them."

Greg turned another page. "KEYGATE of Newtech." His voice dropped. "Jesus, Amore… why are you so interested in Maxwell?"

Amore nodded, his eyes intense. "To some, KEYGATE may appear to be nothing more than a social media platform where individuals create, share, and watch short videos, but it's more. It's surveillance behavior tracking and manipulated outcomes."

Greg's eyebrow rose. "And the public safety component?"

"It is viewed as something a person can enjoy in their spare time," Amore said. "But it's profiling individuals and communities. On average, a user opens the app approximately 17.6 times daily, for at least an hour on the platform. During that time, their data is being traded—to private companies, to overseas entities, even to risk analysis firms. That information is then linked to your profile, which is used to set up an algorithm designed to predict what will supposedly interest you. Each time you dislike or like something, each time you click a pop-up, it makes the data more personalized, to the extent that the algorithm doesn't only know you—it becomes you. When all the data is collected, that's when you don't have any choices anymore. You're cattle being herded. Think about how one day this will be so advanced that it can predict suggested thoughts that had not even materialized yet due to liking a video that can be categorized as "anomalous behaviors" Newtech tracks."

He tapped one of the pages: a signed purchase agreement between Newtech and a third-party analytics group, one of several he found. "And then there's this—predictive policing. AI tools flagging people based on habits, neighborhood density, even social circles."

Greg blinked. "And people consent to this?"

Greg exhaled. "You're not just kicking the hornet's nest—you're punching it."

Amore leaned forward, lowering his voice. "The bad part is most of the devices sold to enhance the app are made from materials that originate in pro-labor states in Eastern Europe with plants of questionable origins. And for some reason, every one of the rivals that try to break into the market gets underpriced, bought out, or sued out of business." Greg let out a low whistle. "So, he's a CEO with a God complex."

"No," Amore said. "He's worse. He's untouchable. Every door to him goes through some NDA, some vanished source, some 'internal restructuring.'" Greg continued reading through the notes and stopped when he reached a particular section. "And the jargon in this report," he said, quoting from a press release. "'Behavioral guidance through integrated pathways.'" He looked up. "You cited BrandPulse Strategies and NinthFrame Media in your framing analysis? Are these from Melanie's past work?"

Amore shrugged. "I asked her for some general PR guidance on messaging weeks ago—nothing to do with this report, just how to navigate editorial roadblocks. Yes, those articles were publicly posted, and yes, they were her past clients, but the phrasing was exactly what I needed to thread the needle. It gave the hook credibility."

Greg lifted an eyebrow, skeptical. "Sure, but they're also two of her old clients. You didn't say her name, but anyone with brains and a search bar will connect the dots."

Amore leaned back, rubbing his eyes. "I needed a good hook: a good, sharp, yet solid one. That phrasing helped me connect the message being conveyed."

Greg sat there for a moment. "You realize what you've done, right? You've included something that can be traced—implied, sure, but traced—back to her."

"She gave me insight, not a quote."

"Doesn't matter," Greg cut in, his jaw clenched in a hard line. "You're going to drag her into a corporate war. It's enough to raise red flags and if this blows up, let's hope she doesn't get hit by the blast radius."

Amore didn't answer right away. He stared at the document in his hands, the lines between professional instinct and personal ties starting to blur.

"I'm not dragging her into this," Amore said. "I'm reporting a story. One I've been researching for a year."

Greg's eyes moved down the page, scanning chunks of the exposé: offshore shell companies, falsified development claims, and political donations funneled through third-party nonprofits. A tangled web that is risky to publish, but too important not to.

"So, you're really doing this," Greg said finally. "This version."

Amore nodded. "Cleanest I've got. Everything else is noise. This one hits."

Greg reclined in his chair, exhaling. He lost the smile and said in a more subdued tone, "Given the length of time spent on this, I've made some judgments on this process. Hell, even bringing me in at the last minute for a final review where countless eyes have been scrutinizing your credibility from the start makes me wonder." With an open-ended pause, he continued, "Truth is, I believe Jim or someone at the paper has been the one holding you back. The resubmissions? The nitpicking? It has the smell of sabotage to it."

Amore looked down at the draft print he had in his hand. "He could be protecting something. Or someone."

Greg nodded. "Probably both."

"Nevertheless," Amore said, "if we pull this off… it's not a headline. It's history."

"You've written big stories before," Greg said. "Actual ones. Policy-changing ones. You don't need this one to matter."

"But I do," Amore said, his voice steady, almost defiant. "I could pretend like everyone else, act like I don't see a wrong that needs to be righted. But the reason I became a reporter in the first place was for the integrity of the truth." He leaned back slightly, a small smile at the corner of his lips. "You want to know what my very first actual investigation was? Figuring out when Santa Claus was going to visit me on Christmas Eve."

Greg snorted and drank his coffee slowly. "Oh yeah? How did that one turn out?"

"As expected," Amore shrugged. "Didn't catch Saint Nick in the act, but I did come away with a new appreciation for my parents."

Greg raised an eyebrow. "Was this before or after you got your lump of coal?"

"Asshole," Amore said with a grin. "It was after."

Greg chuckled, then let out a long breath and shook his head. "You've always been stubborn. And I've always had this weird habit of showing up right when you're about to do something stupid."

"Exactly. Some of your sources? Solid. Others? Could blow up in your face. And Maxwell? He's surrounded by handlers, lawyers, private walls. Guy is like the Teflon Don—nothing sticks."

"So, I'll swing harder," Amore muttered. "I'm not interested in chasing mediocrities."

Amore stood up, gathering his notes, checking his watch. "The meeting's at eleven. Let's see if the truth can get past the gatekeepers. If this won't fly, I have alternatives. There's enough information here to bring down more than Maxwell. I've been pursuing every lead, every dead end. People have been covering up this story. But the truth? It's not going to remain buried."

Greg also rose. "Just remember—once it's out there, you can't take it back."

"Good," Amore replied. "That means I'm doing it right."

"No, you would simply be sane," Greg teased.

Greg rose alongside him. "11 a.m. in the war room. Ready?"

"I was born ready," Amore replied. "Let's see who blinks first."

Chapter 3

The Final Ultimatum

Entering the glass war conference room, the atmosphere felt only slightly less chaotic than the bullpen. The space was filled with suits and a casual yet formal air. It gave off an all-business mindset that masqueraded as just another day at the office. The room brimmed with people from every corner of the company: editorial assistants, senior editors, managing editors, and most importantly, the editor-in-chief, Jim.

As Amore and Greg stepped inside, they could see the subtle choreography; everyone moving in their own fashion either to find a seat or position themselves to pass along information. Colleagues came up offering polite greetings: "Good morning," and "Looking forward to hearing your story." But the words were hollow, carrying no real substance.

Amore had been in this room before, more than once. He could already picture who would be present and on which side they would fall, whether for or against him. The only difference this time was that it truly mattered. There was no going back. Either they would publish his findings or let the story die at the wayside. That thought bubbled in his head as he scanned the room.

There was Allison, the Director Editor. The last time they spoke, she had looked baffled at the points he'd raised. And Charles, an editor who was supportive but often combative. A few others usually agreed with him, but in the end, the one with the most sway was Jim. Jim stood at the head of the table, sleeves rolled up and jaw clenched. He scanned the room of seated editors and reporters, his gaze going deliberately past the screen behind him on which the headline flashed, bold and unremorseful: ***"The Newtech Illusion: Public Safety or Quiet Control?"***

He glared at Amore, looking him straight in the eye. "I don't like it."

Amore shoved his chair back, letting the silence thicken. "Good morning to you too."

Greg quickly moved to dispel the tension. "Good morning, everyone. Let's cut short the introductions and move into the story."

Amore stood before the boardroom, aware that everyone had reviewed his submission. Opening his presentation, he grabbed the presenter remote control and began with the slideshow. It detailed how Maxwell's Newtech had become a giant, using its **Pulse Hub** and **KEYGATE** app to secretly monitor users. Amore's investigation uncovered a data collection program that funneled user behavior into offshore companies. He also exposed Maxwell's anti-competitive practices and evidence of insider trading.

Jim dismissed him. "This story is a minefield, Amore. You're tugging on threads from every angle—data tracking, labor exploitation, predictive policing. It reads more like a manifesto with footnotes than a narrative. We've vetted it, and yeah, the data's there, but the issue remains: Gargon Maxwell is off limits. What you've got on him, as fascinating as it is, won't stand a chance against the kind of legal barrage he'd unleash. He's protected, Amore. A ghost in plain daylight. If we pursue him head-on, it risks everything for the paper. Strong sources do not stop lawsuits, and if we get sued, you're not the one in depositions; we are."

Greg cleared his throat. "It's been vetted and cited. The reports are clean. His sources are deep. Stronger than most we've run with."

Jim glanced at him, then back to Amore. "I know. Doesn't matter. Which is why it's scarier. This story… it feels designed to be explosive."

Amore's eyes narrowed and a smirk touched his lips. "Right. Because protecting the public only counts if no one with money notices."

Jim leaned forward, the sharp angles across his weathered face hardening. His voice cut through the silence—firm, edged with frustration, but not without a hint of concern.

"Look," he began, sifting through the scattered paperwork across the table, his eyes stopping on a page with a detailed flow chart. Amore's meticulous work was undeniable. "We've reviewed everything you've submitted; notes, faxes, redlines, background checks… the whole damn trail. You've clearly put in the work, Amore. No one's disputing that."

He placed the particular page between two fingers, holding it up as if it were heavier than the others. He looked at Amore. "There are lines here worth exploring in the form of data consumption and manipulation. The narrative here is undeniable. But we must determine what's publishable."

Amore's expression twisted, his hands curling into fists in his lap. Jim continued, more emphatically now. "Maxwell doesn't carry weight in this version. No matter how many trails lead back to him, it doesn't change the outcome of the story. He's background noise; high-profile but journalistically and legally, irrelevant."

Amore stood abruptly, the chair scraping against the floor. His voice, though low, bristled with restrained fury. "I've spent over a year on this, Jim. A full goddamn year. I've chased every lead, filed paperwork till my fingers bled, and jumped through hoops just to get stonewalled at every turn. I'm treated like I'm some rogue or liability instead of the one dragging this story to light."

He took a breath, barely steady. "If there wasn't something there, we'd never have ended up here, would we? So why can't we pursue Maxwell? Is it that he's wealthy? Because of his name? Because of his reputation? What is it about him that makes him so untouchable?"

Slowly, Jim turned to him, eyes meeting in a firm, unyielding stare. "The question, Amore, is why are you so damn obsessed with this man."

Silence mounted between them.

"You've got clearance on the bulk of the story," Jim went on, his voice quieter but no less direct. "We've left you some room. But you're stuck on

Maxwell like a dog on a bone. You're not reporting; you're personalizing. You're making this all about you."

He let the words hang there. "Is it ego? Do you want to be the one to break the biggest story of the decade? Or is there something else? Some grudge you're carrying, some hatred for who he is or what he represents?"

Jim exhaled, pushing the file away from him as if he was physically exhausted. "No matter the reason why, the facts remain the same. What you've got on him—it's not quite sufficient enough. You know it. And deep down, I think you know I'm right."

Amore didn't say anything for a second. He stood rigid, fists knotted at his sides, shoulders straining to push out the burden of all that wasn't said. His eyes were burning not with rage, but with the pain of a man who's buried too much for too long. He was looking past Jim, past the walls of the conference room, beyond some invisible point past the glass. When he did speak, his voice was rough, softer now, but every word struck like a blow against stone.

"You think I am concerned with glory?" He slowly shook his head, laughing under his breath, but there was no humor in it. "You think this is about ego? You really think I'd throw a year of my life down the drain on something this broken, this twisted, just so my own name could be in a headline?"

He stepped forward, his voice growing tight, raw. Amore's eyes fell to the file Jim had pushed away, then came back up to meet Jim's. "And you want me to walk away? Call him 'background noise' and focus on the stuff that's easy to print? No. No, that's not journalism. That's cowardice."

Jim's jaw tightened, but he didn't interrupt. Amore went on. "I'm not fixated. I'm convinced. Maxwell isn't just a name on the edge of the story; he's the thread. You pull him, and this whole thing unravels. The reason his involvement feels so thin, the reason so much of this smells like performance: it's because there's a deeper rot, and he's sitting right at the center of it."

He leaned on the edge of the table now, the fire in his voice tempered by something closer to exhaustion. "You say I don't have enough. Fine. But don't lie and say it isn't there. Don't gaslight me into thinking that I'm crazy just because the weight of this man's influence is something no one wants to bear."

He paused, letting the room fall silent once more. Then, softer, practically a whisper: "You're right. I am invested. Because if we don't tell this story the way it's supposed to be told, then what the hell are we doing here?"

Amore's tone dropped. "Let's get this out in the open now. This is not about ethics. It's risk. Jim, I think someone in this paper is actively sabotaging this article. All those documentation requests, the revision demands, edits, fact checks, resubmits. That was not routine procedure. That's a deliberate slow roll."

Jim looked over, tense. "You think someone in the paper is actively sabotaging the article?"

Amore said, his voice cold, "No, Jim. I think someone doesn't just want it delayed. I think someone doesn't want it to exist at all. And they're willing to actively hinder it to ensure that."

Jim didn't flinch. "But this piece? It's dangerous. You're ruffling feathers on every level of the ladder. You've got labor unions, venture capitalists, and now you've managed to tie in public safety and consumer surveillance. You sure you want to walk this plank?"

Amore did not blink. "If I don't share this with the public then what are our jobs as reporters good for? With this forum, we don't just write stories. We are here to shed light on things that are not acceptable in the world."

Slouching forward, elbows on the table, voice low but thick with icy sarcasm, Amore announced, "I just love waking up every morning wondering which NDA I'm going to violate."

"Amore," Jim warned.

"I mean," Amore continued, eyes glinting, "what kind of journalist would I be if I wasn't irrationally chasing corporate corruption while pissing off every advertiser we've ever had?"

Greg sighed into his hand. "Here we go…"

Jim folded his arms. "You've made enemies, Amore. You're making more. That stubborn streak of yours; it doesn't play well when the stakes are this high."

Amore's smirk returned, tighter now. "Then maybe I should just write meaningless fluff about celebrity gossip and internet trends. Keep the advertisers happy. Sleep better at night."

With a loud thud, Jim slapped a hand down on the table, not hard, but firmly. "You don't need to convince me. You need to convince the board. The legal team. All the people in this room who would have to risk their credibility when it goes live. Some of your facts are good—some of them are hearsay. And Maxwell? He is someone who may be out of reach."

"I'm not selling anything," Amore replied. "I'm here to tell the truth which is my job as a journalist. If the truth needs an ad campaign and a safety net to survive, then maybe it's not the truth people are scared of, but the accountability."

The word "accountability" hung in the air of his mind as a declaration. But beneath the bravado, a flicker of doubt stirred. He thought of Melanie and a moment crept in: the casual way he'd asked for guidance weeks ago. Guidance. He hadn't intended to draw her in, hadn't thought about the level of involvement that Greg had cautioned him against. His principles were made of steel, but the vision of her being caught up in any fallout that may come made him flinch. He clenched his jaw, pushing the uninvited thought away. He had to have faith his meticulous work would be enough to protect her.

Jim studied him for a long beat. "You've covered big stories before. Ones that matter. That have an impact. But this one has both teeth and claws. If you are wrong, even if one part of this fails, then you just don't lose your credibility; you will take the paper down with you."

"And if I'm right?" Amore's voice rose to a low, sharp edge.

Jim's jaw twitched. "Then you still lose. Because you'll have taken out a man half this country doesn't even know controls their lives. And that kind of publicity doesn't come without blowback."

Amore's gaze held steady. "Then I guess I'll take an umbrella."

Jim took a deep breath and turned away, his expression a mix of frustration and resignation. He then looked back at Amore, a look of grim determination on his face. "I'm giving you until Thursday to provide me with something on Maxwell that isn't hearsay. A new angle, a new source, something tangible. If you can do that, we'll talk. If not, this story stays on the table to die." He then turned and left the room without another word.

As Jim left, so did everyone else, leaving Greg and Amore still sitting at the table to gather their belongings.

Greg leaned back in his chair, taking a slow breath. "You just can't help yourself, can you?"

Amore rose, holding his folder. "What would I be if I weren't me?"

Greg shook his head with a faint, bitter smile. "Dumb, suicidal, and no sense, just your principles."

Amore shot him a look. "Those are my best qualities."

"You know," Greg said, rubbing his forehead. "You could still build this out through the affiliates. Cut your losses on Maxwell for the moment. Save the paper. Live to fight another day."

Amore leaned forward, his face held firm in a defiant look. "Why would I do that? I spent months tracking down leads that went nowhere and hours of digging to make sure this wasn't just some made-up story targeting someone in power. What would I be if I didn't go for the big one? This is the one that matters."

For Amore, this is not just a story; it's a crusade. A chance to lay to rest the myth of Gargon Maxwell: no visionary, but a deceiver clothed in innovation and shielded by an entanglement of global complications.

Chapter 4

Beyond Reach

A late afternoon autumn breeze rustled through the trees in Fairview Park.

Footsteps moved slowly along the thoroughfare as Amore stepped out onto the gravel walking trail. The slight crunch of each stone beneath his boots made him feel almost grounded. He needed something concrete to hold onto in a life that had otherwise become anything but stable.

He stumbled upon an empty stone bench facing out to the quaint spot amidst the scenery. Clearing his mind in the peacefulness, he sat, tapping the heel of his shoe against the pavement in a nervous habit. He had arrived early—instinct, maybe, or a desire for a moment of solitude. His eyes followed every passerby, whether it was a couple walking together or someone running with their dog. It was not until he spotted the familiar face of Greg that his eyes lit up, approaching him with that very same uneven stride that was half-confident, half-preoccupied.

"You really made me come out here for this, Amore?" Greg asked, stuffing his hands into his coat pockets. "A public park, middle of the day? Why not a nice café?"

"Took you long enough. Don't you just love getting some fresh air occasionally?" Amore said, rising. "Meeting me in public now, it's like a cheap date."

Greg retorted, "More like I am a friend with benefits. At least you can wine and dine me first?"

Amore smiled, nodding his head toward the empty walking path ahead. "Only kind I can afford these days. Just visiting an old friend, while also trying to keep my last two dollars as well."

That made Greg laugh. It was one of his dry, witty jokes that Amore alone could get away with. They bumped shoulders briefly, the way men do when too much time has passed since they last met, but not enough time to end their connection. Their bond was still strong; it may have been tested, but it was still there.

They eased onto a nearby bench in a more secluded area with fewer people. Both men sat proudly in the awkwardness of the moment like men too tired to argue, but too proud not to jab. "It's been a while since we've talked," Greg said cautiously, his tone measured but laced with something unspoken.

"You've been busy," Amore replied, leaning back. "Still grinding it out at The Inquisitor."

Greg gave a small nod, looking up at the sky, his eyes searching for the words to say. "And you've been busy in your own right. Didn't you start up your own journalism company or something? What is it called again?" His question hung in the air, stained with childlike amusement, maybe even pride.

"If I didn't know better, you'd seem almost believable. You know the name of my company," Amore said in a flat voice. "It's called Beyond Reach. Been running it ever since I walked away."

"Right," Greg said, snapping his fingers as if the memory had just landed. "You launched it about six months after leaving The Inquisitor, right? Built it from the ground up. Organic. Real. It's like watching someone leave home to find their own path." He hesitated, then added, "You've done well, Amore."

Amore studied him to see if Greg was being genuine. "Thanks. We've done more than good. Within a short space of time, we built something meaningful for real journalism, which is unfiltered. I have had to build an entire team of journalists that want to not be controlled on what they can or can't pursue." With a small chuckle, "I even pulled a few good people from The Inquisitor."

Greg smiled, but there was tension beneath it. "Yeah. That part stung. Sometimes you pay a price when others feel the same as you do but don't have the means to express themselves."

"I gave you the offer to join with me; to build this before when we started," Amore shot back, his tone lowering. "At the start, I wanted you by my side. Told you so. But you stayed."

Greg looked away for a moment, jaw locked. "I stayed because I thought it was the right move. Years of life that I created there, it was something that I just can't walk away from. I had responsibilities, not to mention a family. Connections. The Inquisitor had reach, stability… and a hell of a budget. Freedom is not always free."

"I wasn't asking for convenience," Amore said quietly. "I was asking for conviction."

Greg sighed. "You know as well as I do, it's never easy. I couldn't choose between my friendship and the job—not then. That's why I did give you space when you left. I knew you needed that. And maybe… maybe I needed that too."

Amore slowly nodded. "I can understand that you didn't reach out, at least not openly. You just kept tabs from a distance. And I did the same thing. It's a two-way street. But I'm glad we're having this conversation finally."

Greg leaned forward, his face easing. "So am I. Despite everything, I always respected what you were building."

Amore gave a small, dry smile.

Amore continued, asking, "Why did you request a meeting on such short notice? I love the scenery, but I hope you're not planning to eliminate me mafia-style."

"Don't make me have to," Greg said, pulling a folded file from his coat pocket and placing it on his lap.

Amore glanced at it but didn't grab it.

Avoiding eye contact, Greg said, "Before we get into that; have you talked to Melanie lately? How is she doing?"

There was a silence between them that lingered in the air.

"She's good," Amore answered casually. "She is doing better… without me messing things up."

"We text. Birthdays. Holidays. The occasional 'You still breathing?' She's fine."

Greg nodded. "Still doing PR?"

"Yeah. And still too good for me."

Greg started to speak, but Amore cut in, his voice low. "I nearly cost her everything," he went on after a moment. "Her career, her reputation. All for standing up for me when Maxwell's story broke. She stood by me until it started costing her too. I couldn't make her pay for my crusade."

"You still love her."

Amore didn't say anything. He allowed his gaze to drop to the ground. He understood that Greg wasn't asking; he was telling.

"So," Greg broke the silence, "Jim's retiring."

Amore raised a brow. "Seriously?"

Greg nodded. "End of the quarter. Rumor has it he's only hanging around to get through some internal transitions. His replacement's already in the works."

Greg shrugged. "Paper's going digital. He even said, while talking about you one day, that the place doesn't breathe the same life into it without you. You were the glue that held the paper together; one of the best investigative minds we had. Until you weren't."

Amore's chin firmed. "Don't," he warned. "Don't pretend like I left in his good graces. Jim did not care for me at all. This boils down to what

I did. I did what everyone wanted me to do; no, what everyone expected me to do."

Greg said, "What do you mean?"

Raising his voice, Amore continued, "Don't you act like you don't know what I'm talking about. I decided to choose the safe path that would help get the Maxwell story published. I exposed secondary contractors associated with forced labor: anonymous shell firms laundering funds into political tech races. I wrote about companies no one could pronounce until I made them household names."

Intensifying his response, Greg clarified, "And people took notice, which brought much-needed attention to various areas in your report. The more articles you wrote, the more people became aware of issues regarding Newtech."

"Sure," nodded Amore, "did the Post. And so did the Times. They dissected my pieces, quote by quote. One called me 'narrative manipulation under the guise of transparency.' Another used the phrase 'theatrical suspicion disguised as journalism' to describe my work. And those were the good ones. They ruined my reputation and labeled me crazy, manufacturing the Newtech centerpiece as a smear campaign for recognition. And instead of defending me, everyone did what I did; folded and played it safe."

Greg tilted his head to the side. "They crucified you."

Amore dryly laughed. "Not only that, but they copied and crucified me. Half of the stuff they dismissed from my report helped set the stage for their own exposés a year later."

Greg paused, then said softly, "That was your crucible. It legitimized and pushed you to create Beyond Reach. You made it through."

"I did," Amore agreed. "But you know what it cost me."

"I can only imagine, but" Greg was hesitant in his response. "But what?" Amore snapped.

"But I told you to let it go, but you wouldn't," Greg said, matching his tone. "You wouldn't let go. You had every chance to focus on another story. Start somewhere else with another centerpiece, even if it meant taking a step back."

"I do not chase ladders. I build my own. I gave them the biggest story of my life, and they threw it into the shredder," Amore shot back.

Greg, challenging him, said, "You gave them a theory, not a story. Maybe it was the truth, but it wasn't ready yet. You know that."

Amore's voice grew cold. "No, what I know is they were afraid. Advertisers, investors—Gargon's fingers are everywhere. And when the story didn't fit the narrative, it became too dangerous."

Greg glared at him. "And now?"

"Now I run Beyond Reach," Amore said. "A nonprofit investigative news organization that I am a co-founder and editor of."

They both fell silent for a moment, their emotions stewing within them.

"You ever think about coming back?" Greg asked.

"To what?"

"To real journalism."

Amore stood. "Real journalism never left me. But I left the machine that had to be oiled with silence."

"Hardheaded as ever," Greg muttered.

"That's why you keep me around," Amore retorted. "A friend with benefits."

They laughed again, only this time more genuine, breaking the tension between each other.

Turning their attention back to the sealed envelope that sat in Greg's lap, Greg said, "I need your help. This one's different. This is information regarding the girl who was discovered in the Levinson Grand. You've probably seen the reports on the news, but there's more to it. Rumors are going around about a private event two weeks ago involving entertainment moguls, politicians, and influencers. A girl overdosed. Dead. Nothing too official in the media. Everything buried."

"Hardly," Amore answered, cocking an eyebrow before relaxing again. "Word spread in the local papers as an overdose. Horrible, but little surprising for a high-profile hotel like that."

"Yeah," Greg said, rubbing his chin. "That's what I thought too. But there's more chatter under the surface. It's quiet, but loud, if you know where to listen. Like the news wants to break it—without breaking it."

Amore squinted at him. "Sounds like you're describing every story now."

Greg nodded, not disagreeing. "Media outlets ran with the standard narrative: young woman, unknown guests, prescription cocktail, end of story. But I have a few people digging around into it, but nothing concrete yet. There are a couple of whispers that say it wasn't just a party. That hotel's no stranger to high-profile guests. No cameras were working that night. No guest lists. No one is coming forward claiming to know too much about her."

"And let me guess," Amore said, resting his cheek on his hand, "no one's talking from the hotel either."

"Not even anonymously. And the craziest thing? Every time someone tries to push further into the story, something stalls. A cold source, a silent manager, an email thread that disappears."

Amore didn't answer right away. "You think it has to do with something bigger?" he finally asked.

Greg leaned back and exhaled. "I think… it feels bigger. But it's slippery. If you're asking whether I've got the bones of a conspiracy here— no, not yet. But if you're asking whether it's worth looking into?" He gave Amore a look. "Then yeah. It's worth it."

Amore stroked his beard, thinking. "I've heard the rumors, too. But to my eyes, it's just another sad overdose in an unfortunate event."

Greg looked at him. "But it bothers you."

Amore lifted his head, deliberately.

Greg smiled faintly. "I know you, man. You wouldn't have brought it up if you didn't already feel something was wrong."

Amore let out a sigh, but it wasn't irritation—it was weariness over curiosity. "What do you want from me, Greg?"

"Answers," Greg said. "Just to look into it. If not for the story, then maybe for her family. Nobody's giving them answers. I have people looking into it, but they are no Amore Reyes. If you do happen to come up with anything—anything at all—I'll push it through the right channels. Quiet if that's what it has to be. But I'd like to know what happened."

Amore didn't answer right away, a consideration passing through his head. "Send me what you've got," he said to Greg at last. "I'm not promising anything, but I'll take a look."

Greg slid the thin envelope to Amore. "Already on it."

Amore looked at it. "Of course you are."

Greg smiled. "Old habits."

Amore rose, tucking the envelope into his jacket pocket. "Let's just hope this one doesn't get me sued."

Greg glanced upwards. "Wouldn't be a real investigation if it wasn't."

"No coverage at all?" Amore asked.

"Not a word, but there is buzz. You've got a couple of sources in place. When you break it, I'll give you legs from my end."

Amore nodded, balancing the envelope in his palms. "Like the good old days."

Greg smiled. "You lay the groundwork. I smooth out the road."

They stood.

They separated on a half-laugh. Amore shoved the envelope into his jacket as he turned to leave.

"You need to stop playing and have a talk with Melanie," Greg said once more.

Amore shook his head. "She still loves me. But it's complicated. I feel her resentment, her fear, and it is all because of me. I can't fix it with her until I make it right."

Greg said no more. They exchanged a nod and parted ways.

Chapter 5

The First-Time Guest

The building that housed Beyond Reach didn't look like much. It matched the personality of its occupants with its brick face in a row of sand-blasted warehouses repurposed as "creative spaces." Nestled above a repurposed old bookstore on a sedate corner block, a brass plaque displayed the name. Inside, the space was something else: warm, with sleek hardwood floors, and glass compartments that created a sense of precise control. The waiting room was minimalist but refined, decorated in soft grays and navy blue, the kind of color that expressed restraint and consideration. The glow of three mismatched lamps and the soft sound of an old record player playing Coltrane provided the therapeutic mood within the space. There were books on the wall, which included memoirs of investigations, censored reports, and court transcripts. What stood out the most was a small plaque behind the counter that read: **Facts Don't Flinch**. A framed painting by a local artist of a typewriter hung on the wall, a nod to a profession rapidly losing its ink and soul.

Amore walked into Beyond Reach's office building, the weight of his conversation with Greg still clinging to him like humidity.

Naima sat at the reception desk, legs crossed, typing away on her laptop as she propped the phone on her shoulder. Displaying her usual no-nonsense expression, her curls were tied back in a loose knot.

"Yes, he's back. No, you can't just drop by… Because that's just not the way we do things anymore. Send me the breakdown via email. Thanks."

She glanced up as Amore came in. "Greg?" she asked in a questioning tone.

Amore shrugged. "Always ten percent information, ninety percent theatrics."

"You have someone waiting in your office," she went on, her voice falling slightly. "Said he had an appointment. But I double-checked the appointment book, and you didn't have anything scheduled. I checked his ID, and his name is Lucius Vale. Wouldn't say much more."

"What?" Amore asked, bewildered.

"The guy. Said he knew you from past acquaintances. Said you were expecting him."

"I wasn't expecting anyone."

Amore froze mid-step. "And you just let him in?"

Naima shrugged, finally looking up. "I didn't just wave him through. Security's watching him. I've had my finger on the silent alarm the whole time. If he so much as blinked wrong, Darnell would've had him cuffed in under thirty seconds. He was... polite. Calm. Something about him just seemed nonthreatening. He didn't seem like a lunatic. He seemed like someone who knew more than he let on."

"I'll take it from here," Amore stated, his tone cautious.

Amore exhaled and moved down the narrow hallway to his office. The glass door was wedged open just slightly. Inside, a man stood against the bookshelf, admiring a framed headline from Amore's Informative days.

"You have more courage than you realize," Amore stated flatly, closing the door behind him. "Lucius, I presume?"

The man slowly turned. Tall, thin, in dark charcoal pants and a tight but worn turtleneck under his coat. His eyes were sharp, measured.

"You carry your past well," Lucius said, pointing at the framed newspaper clipping. "The Politician's Daughter. That was one hell of a takedown."

Amore did not smile. "I'm not here for compliments. You're not the first person to wander in here expecting to impress me with citations. Let's get straight to the point. What do you want?" He took a seat at his desk but kept his hand on the top of his drawer where he kept his own safeguards nestled in leather and steel.

"I am a long-time reader, but a first-time guest," Lucius said.

Amore pressed harder. "You've got thirty seconds before I call security."

They gazed at each other for a very long time. And then Lucius raised his hands and smiled. "No need. I am not here to fight. Just… align interests."

"Align interests?" Amore said, irritated.

"I read your past works," Lucius continued. "Even prior to Beyond Reach. Your exposé on the Marsen Youth Shelter cover-up? Genius. You were a presence in bringing down that facility. And then the Bonhurst Insurance fraud ring. That had grit. You made enemies, but you didn't flinch. That's rare."

"Flattery again."

"No. Respect."

Amore's eyes narrowed. "So why now? Why approach me?"

"I've been following your work. Particularly the Maxwell case."

Amore's body stiffened.

"Funny," said Lucius. "That name once opened doors. Now it gets you onto a blacklist."

"I'm listening," Amore responded, not dropping his guard.

"I was on the same track," Lucius said. "Three years ago. I was quieter about it, slowly building up the story. Private circles. Leaks through whispers. I got too close. It was the story that never reached the edit desk. It was buried… and I got buried with it, too. And like you, I got burned. Lost my column, my clearance, even my marriage."

He moved his weight slowly, in a non-threatening way. "You and I have been dancing around the same issue. Two dogs on the same scent, just at different angles."

Amore glared at him sharply. "So why now?"

Amore stood firm. "You want me to believe that you tracked me down because we shared a boogeyman?"

Watching Lucius closely, he replied in a mocking tone, "That story is already done and closed. We published multiple articles on Maxwell and his affiliates. You know as well as I do that everything connected to that story has already been established. So why would I revisit something that's already been said?"

Lucius smirked. "Because you came close. You almost brought the man down for what he's done. I've read all your stories. Yes, you managed to hit a few of his entities, but don't you want to take down the man himself? The head of the snake? He may seem untouchable, but he can be exposed."

Amore shook his head, with more bitterness than amusement. "That's all well and good. But that's the past. My objective now is whatever I'm working on and not chasing a man I've already chased."

"I'm not asking you to reopen old wounds," Lucius said. "I'm offering you a thread. You can pull it or not."

"And what makes you think I need your thread?"

Lucius's voice grew softer as he leaned forward. "Because from what I have found, his involvement in the world is greater than you can imagine. And I can't do it alone."

"And now you're requesting what from me?" Amore asked.

"To trade notes. Maybe collaborate. You're good, Amore. But you're still working in the light. Maxwell's empire lies in the shadows."

Lucius didn't move. "I'm not your enemy. I'm just a man who's tired of chasing this alone."

"Prove it."

Lucius smiled but just barely. "I will. In time. For now, take this." He pulled a thin, cream-colored business card from his jacket. He placed it gently on Amore's desk. It had no name, just a symbol: a black hourglass wrapped in copper wire.

"You will know what it is when the time's right. If you call me, we can start connecting the dots. If not, you don't have to worry about seeing me again." Lucius paused at the door. "You know the sad thing is we're the last ones who care what's real in this world while others will accept the lie more easily. If you decide you want more information," he said, "call me. Or don't."

Then, without another word, he departed the office.

Amore stared at the card long after the door closed, the symbol etched into his memory. Outside the office, Naima's voice floated faintly from her desk to Amore. She muttered under her breath, "I still don't trust him."

Neither did Amore. But the card sat there on the desk like an itch on the edge of his mind, one that would only get worse with time. Pondering to himself, he didn't know whether he had found himself an ally or stepped into the mouth of something bigger than he could understand.

One thing was sure: he'd just unintentionally come across a door to something that was unresolved within him, which had wanted to be revealed for a very long time.

Chapter 6

Who Are You

Amore sat in the dark silence of his office; the only sound that could be heard was the muffled buzz from the ceiling lights. Lucius's appearance had made more than an impression; it had raised questions that struggled in the back of his mind. The name Gargon Maxwell ruminated in his thoughts. It was as if the man had just walked into his office—flashing that wide smile, laughing straight at him. Months of chasing every lead, pushing through every setback, now rose up and mocked him, bringing back the disappointment, the rage, and worst of all, the humiliation he endured after publishing his so-called centerpiece.

Anything tied to Maxwell opened wounds he could never fully close. But what cut deepest was the man who had reopened the door—the one who led him back down this path, forcing him to relive the shadow of the man who had taken everything from him: Lucius Vale. Who the hell was this man?

He'd run the name "Lucius Vale" through his memory in the last hour. In over a decade of tracing tips, sitting in courtrooms, and dissecting backroom deals, he could count on one hand the number of times he had seen that name appear as a byline. Hardly ever, if ever. And yet, there'd been a feeling of familiarity in the man's demeanor—that of a veteran journalist, sharp, specific, and layered like someone who'd done this too long to play dumb.

"Naima," he instructed.

His assistant cracked open the frosted glass door about halfway, tablet in hand. "I was expecting you to call about him," she said. "Already checked. Nothing recent under his name. But I did find some older contributor threads. He either ghostwrote or at least assisted with some longform writing attached to *The Baltimore Eye* and a syndicate piece in *The Indelible* a couple of years back."

"That's something. Keep digging. I need to know everything you can find on Mr. Vale," Amore muttered. He twirled Lucius's business card in his fingers—black card stock, silver-lettered font, the phrase beneath his name: Proof lives in the footnotes.

Naima stood in the doorway. "You know, I almost didn't let him in."

"You did the right thing. Security was watching him the whole time?"

"Since he stepped through the lobby. I didn't see his name in today's log, which alarmed me at first, but he had clearance credentials from the *Union Guild*. Legitimate. Old, but legitimate. Against my best judgment, I made the assumption it was an error but should have trusted my gut. Still had my finger near the panic button." She frowned.

Preoccupied with the card in his hand, he spoke. "I trust you, but next time don't leave me in the dark." His tone was understanding, yet sounded almost as if he were a parent disappointed with their child. He still understood the danger that she could have put herself in as well.

"I never do," Naima said. As she walked toward the door, Amore added, "I'll be unavailable the rest of the day. If anyone asks, I'm out indefinitely."

Naima raised a brow. "You planning to go dark?"

"Just deep."

She closed the door behind her without a word.

Amore opened the manila envelope he had received from Greg earlier. A cascade of printed photographs spilled across his desk. A woman stared back at him from every angle. Early thirties, maybe late twenties. Dark hair and chiseled features. The first photo was a commercial headshot with a flawless pose. The rest were unscripted: blurred, cluttered, candid. The final photos he viewed caused shudders in his gut. She sat in a bathtub, head thrown back, a few strands of hair drifting in bathwater. Pill bottles and an untouched glass of champagne lined the tile floor.

The young woman looking back at him from the photo was named Lisa Thompson.

Looking deeply into her photo, there was something that stood out: her hazel eyes. Childlike in their openness, yet laced with a deeper allure, the glee of their presence showcased a life that had seen too much too quickly and refused to let the weight of it show.

Amore flipped through the scattered images of her life. Each moment highlighted different phases of her personality; some spontaneous but candid, some posed for social media, but all were her, yet diverse. They spanned years and points, each with its own appearance: glittering nights at rooftop lounges, winter mornings under giant sweaters, backstage moments full of laughter, and rare but selected moments of solitude in introspective portraits. Through all of them, however, one constant remained: Lisa carried an aura about her. She lived loudly, brightly, as if she was chasing each moment before it could vanish. She was vibrant, flamboyant, starving to be the center of it all and yet, there was something missing. Or perhaps something was hidden.

He studied the curve of her smile in one photo, the tilt of her head in another. It was becoming clear. A picture isn't the truth; it's just a version of one. It's a mask, chosen or imposed upon her, that she'd wear to convey a certain impression. And the more he scanned each picture, the more the mask appeared to tighten over Lisa. His instincts, honed by years of journalism, flared with unease.

"Who are you, really?" he murmured aloud to no one.

This felt like it was not just another tragic overdose. A young woman found dead in a hotel bathtub poses too many questions with little to no answers; that does not make enough sense. For no reason at all? No. Something wasn't right. Death is rarely random when drugs, fame, and secrecy are part of the picture. Who gave her the drugs? Why? When? Was

she alone, or doubtful? If it was an overdose, then was she meant to die—
or was her death merely a collateral casualty?

He rested back against his chair, fingers intertwined, the weight of
those unresolved questions weighing on his mind like unseen pressure.
Piquing his interest, all the variables were intriguing. Lisa was someone who
had her whole life in front of her. The potential was there, and if she had
been given the opportunity, who knows how far she could have gone? Her
life mirrored who she was, but Amore couldn't help but think to himself
how sad it was. This doesn't give him what he wants: the true person behind
the mask. Then, quietly but firmly, he spoke, "I need more on her.
Everything. Who she was… and what she was doing to cause this."

"Naima!" he shouted. "Can you get me more information on Lisa
Thompson?"

Responding quickly, "I can begin pulling all the archives from personal
records to start," she said. Naima, sharp-eyed and vigilant, would begin
tracking her every step by pulling archived references, social connections,
security access logs, even rental car receipts tied to Lisa's name. But
Amore's fascination wasn't purely procedural; it felt more personal now.
There was something about this case that crawled under his skin.

The photos of Lisa's body, submerged in the water of the tub, did not
serve Amore, as they only showcased her in a gruesome light. He needed
to feel the presence of the room where her body was found; more presence
than photos could offer. He needed to see the room for himself to gain a
clearer indication. The emotions and curiosity peaked within him. He had
to observe the scene himself. But the Levinson Grand Hotel was still
crawling with law enforcement and PR personnel, each tighter mouthed
than the previous one. It would be too reckless to approach directly. He
couldn't be a bull charging into a crowd. He had to be indirect; quiet,
watching, weaving through the environment without causing attention.

No reservation under her name. No check-in history. And yet she'd
been found dead in a suite said to house foreign officials and studio moguls.
The hotel's PR had launched into full erasure mode. Only one

entertainment blog had mentioned the accident, but it was only three lines buried in an article about failed Hollywood parties.

Amore rubbed his jaw, eyes scanning the details. A private event had been held the same night. The guest list was sealed. No photos, no statements, no fallout. He needed a way in.

Later that afternoon, Naima handed him a keycard in a discreet leather sleeve.

"Room's booked under my name. Seventh floor. Said you're my cousin visiting from Portland."

"You always make it easy."

"I make it discreet."

He nodded and left without saying another word.

Chapter 7

Levinson Grand Hotel

uxury was the defining feature of the Levinson Grand Hotel, a cornerstone of downtown. Its name radiated wealth. From the doormen posted at the entrance in their black tuxedos, their posture crisp and their greetings rehearsed, to the valet parking attendants who appeared the moment you pulled up, every aspect of the hotel was designed to make every guest feel like royalty.

Onlookers would often enter the enormous lobby just to glimpse the aura of the hotel, which was decked out with ballrooms and an expensive restaurant where entrées cost more than most could afford. It was very much the kind of place people adored being seen in, even if they couldn't imagine actually staying there.

Seizing the opportunity, Naima booked his reservation at an ideal time, when people were continuously coming and going. It became apparent that Lisa's death had generated a buzz in the city. People who hadn't even known of the hotel's existence before now flocked to its doors just to catch a glimpse or see what had happened. Entering the building, the lobby air lingered with the scent of citrus and bleach; a virtual waterfall flowed, streaming down the marble wall next to the elevators. Amore navigated through the area with purpose, barely acknowledging the concierge who appeared occupied with a Bluetooth headset in his ear. He had walked the grounds in advance, mapping the hotel layout in his mind: staff entrances, housekeeping and janitor rooms, fire escapes—every inch. Even though the investigation was still ongoing, and the crime scene at the hotel had already been viewed and examined, there were still lingering traces of the case. He recognized the section of the ballroom closed for "maintenance," the corridor subtly roped off with police tape. Suite 802 hadn't been thoroughly cleaned. No surprise there. Knowing he would be unable to proceed directly in this area, it was best to fish for information and see what he could gauge from the staff.

He made his way to the front desk, keeping his voice calm but tinged with irritation. "Hi, yeah—I'm staying in 716. I didn't get towels when I checked in. And the turn-down service… wasn't five-star, exactly."

The manager emerged in minutes. Slicked hair, firm smile, eyes full of repressed tension. "So sorry, sir. Let me personally make sure it's addressed. We pride ourselves on hospitality."

Amore's smile relaxed, a feigned appreciation. "Thank you ever so much! Glad to hear that you still value customer service so highly." He moved forward, a casual whisper. "Also… saw one of the upper rooms taped off. A bit difficult not to notice. Hope everything's okay."

The man's smile faltered just slightly. "Sorry, sir, I'm not free to talk about that. Hotel policy."

"Oh, sure," Amore said, feigning amusement. "Didn't want to get caught in anything… bad publicity and all that."

"Makes sense."

The manager, though friendly and polite by nature in his role, had clearly grown tired of answering questions about the apparent death under his watch. Even when the subject was only hinted at, his attitude and demeanor turned short and snippy. Amore quickly realized that pressing him further would not be in his best interest.

They exchanged shallow small talk. Nothing more. Amore left without following through.

Heading up to his room, Amore went with calm intention. There was always a method behind his madness. He had specifically requested this room; the identical replica of the one Lisa was found dead in just days earlier. The staff, not having any notion as to why he needed it, had given it to him readily. Not having access to the actual scene had been unthinkable, but mimicking the space to the best of their ability gave him something most journalists never had: perspective.

Photographs alone could only do so much. They minimized a moment, but what he required was immersion.

He swiped his keycard, entered, and softly shut the door behind him.

Immediately, the scent of expensive linen and polished marble greeted him. The suite smelled of lavishness—plush carpeted floors, a modern kitchen with chrome appliances to the left, and a soft ambient glow from hidden lighting beneath the cabinetry. He walked past the kitchen, barely noticing it, and walked into the bedroom.

A king-sized bed stood centered in front of a textured velvet wall, covered in pristine white linens and accompanied by sleek nightstands. The room radiated high-dollar elegance—cool-toned with subtle golden accents, the sort of space designed to encourage guests to forget that the outside world was even real. But Amore had not come for the luxury.

He approached the bathroom.

Marble tile. Spotless countertops. A rainfall shower. Every luxury had been accounted for, but the bathtub anchored him to the spot. It was the same model as the one in the scene shots. He sat beside it, his arm bracing himself on the edge of the tub. In his mind, he retraced the crime scene from the water, the faint ring of bubbles, her corpse slumped with her head twisted, as if unnaturally.

There was something odd about the angle of her head.

To the naked eye, it might have been a common slouch in death. But to Amore, it seemed off. Almost posed. Staged.

He crept into the tub slowly, clothed, and slipped down into roughly the same position as in the photographs. Cold. Unyielding. He mimicked the angle, turning his head at the same angle Lisa's had been. This is what he saw from this position. He imagined what she may have seen, what her last moments could have been.

"Futile," he considered, an empty gesture. Was he only chasing a story, constructing conclusions from his own thoughts?

But then something had alarmed him.

A detail in the crime scene photos hadn't fully registered until now. A glass of champagne resting on the edge of the tub It hadn't tipped, spilled, or shattered, but its placement and the angle were all wrong for a natural fall. Still retaining some fluid. And not run-of-the-mill champagne; this was vintage, this was luxurious. Even with all of the luxuries of the Levinson Grand, this bottle wasn't in its stock. This wasn't some complimentary minibar bottle, either, or part of the hotel's basic offerings. If she had that champagne, someone had either brought it with them or ordered it in advance. But the angle… the placement of the bottle and glass didn't line up with where her body had been found. If she had slumped, the glass should've tipped, spilled, shattered maybe. But it hadn't.

The scene was off.

Amore slowly climbed out of the tub, his thoughts racing. It was a subtle but vital inconsistency—the kind that could change everything.

He grabbed his phone, scribbled out a quick reminder, and then quickly left the room as he came in.

Chapter 8

The Lead

A surge of energy coursed through his body. It was a heightened sense of finding something that could be relevant to this story. Amore's thoughts spiraled in his head—the champagne bottle. How could they have missed it? How could it have been overlooked? How was such a small detail not even considered? Perhaps it was considered, and he just didn't know. Either way, he had to get back to the office. By the time he arrived, Naima should already have something of importance pulled up for Lisa.

He skirted through the halls and got on the elevator, anxious but trying not to show it, making his way down to the lobby. He exited the elevator, but a flow of people was still pouring in. He cut through the crowd to make it to the exit. As he got closer, a voice rang out, "Sir? Sir? Hold on a minute." He shuffled, unsure if the voice was meant for him. He looked around and noticed it was the hotel manager calling him back. Not wanting to appear suspicious—though it probably wouldn't matter—he slowly walked up to him.

"Yes?"

"I just wanted to follow up with you to see if you were able to get the complimentary towels. My staff came to your room but was unable to reach you. They said there appeared to be a slight commotion."

Amore felt a jolt of anxiety. Did they know? Was this a test? Turning on his pleasantness, he quickly assured the manager there was no issue, that he wanted to rest, and that he had received the towels; everything was fine.

Cutting the conversation short, he said flatly, "I would have loved to stay and talk more, but I have to go."

The manager then said, "You're right. I understand. I just wanted to ensure that everything was OK."

"Everything is, thank you." He quickly proceeded to the exit.

As he walked out the doors, individuals poured in and out in great waves. As he started to move, he took notice of certain people walking in the same direction as him. Was someone following him? He thought maybe he was just being paranoid, but the more he walked toward his car, the greater the feeling grew. It was as if something was telling him someone was there, almost like a spider sense.

Even though it was just a feeling, he couldn't help but watch all the people around him. Bystanders who were obvious, like families and those clearly not headed in his direction, were no threat, but there was one man who stood out from the rest: genuinely striking in his appearance. Even though he could have passed for just another person, his demeanor suggested otherwise. Every movement carried the sense that he was more interested in Amore, as if he were watching to see where he would go. It wasn't late, but it was enough to make him wonder. He had noticed him earlier, when he was speaking to the manager, but that could have been a coincidence. Then again, coincidences didn't happen often.

People were going in different directions and were entitled to do so. It was one of the busiest times, but he had to shake the feeling off. Cautiously, he began changing his pattern to see if someone was there: going in and out of businesses, stopping and going, acting as if he was window shopping at times. This helped ease the feeling. He knew he could not do this all day; if he was being followed, he would need to end it because he couldn't keep this up. Within moments, he began to jog, then gradually run and sprint to see if anyone would keep up. When he finally slowed down, his doubts eased. He was assured that there wasn't anyone there, but he needed to make it to the office. He made it back to his vehicle and then proceeded to where he needed to go.

Arriving at his office, mixed emotions ran through him. The unease of possibly being followed lingered, but he pushed those concerns aside. What mattered most was the discovery of the champagne bottle, the detail that refused to leave his mind. As he walked through the lobby, he greeted Naima.

"How are you looking on the information for Lisa?"

"I've pulled general information from her social media feeds and public records. It's on your desk," she replied.

"Excellent." He proceeded to make his way into his office.

Looking over the information, he asked himself, "Where to start?" The $500 bottle of champagne found in the bathroom where she died. To a casual observer, it might have seemed like an extravagant party that took a wrong turn. But to Amore, it immediately waved a warning sign. The champagne wasn't on the hotel's menu—wasn't even carried there. That simple fact raised a bigger question: Where did it come from? And why was it left behind with a dead woman in a luxury suite?

One possibility was that Lisa or other guests brought it in themselves. But that opened up a whole new line of inquiry: What local vendors carried it? Who bought it? And what occasion, if any, was it connected to?

Amore was trained to go beyond, to follow what others did not notice. The more he investigated Lisa's past, the more contradictions surfaced. She was an aspiring intern in broadcast media, who worked behind the scenes at various sports and entertainment events. Her role was more operational than glamorous, which could explain her connection to high-end venues. But it didn't explain how she ended up in this particular suite, surrounded by expensive alcohol and trace amounts of designer drugs. Her reported income simply didn't match the lifestyle on display.

Amore turned to her social media for clues. The majority of the posts were innocent enough: family snapshots, group photos, moments that appeared genuine. But scattered throughout them were flashes of a different life. A nightlife. Scrolling back to the days before her death, Amore found a video that stopped him in his tracks. Lisa was outside a nightclub, surrounded by a buzzing crowd. Someone shouted off-camera: "We're about to take over this place! We're outside! We're alive!"

In the video, a young woman—petite, feisty—held the identical brand of champagne found at the crime scene, smiling and posing with it for the camera. Her name was tagged in the post: Catalina Gomez.

Amore's journalistic instincts flared. Catalina was not necessarily a guest; she could just be a random partygoer. But she had been with Lisa that night, and possibly on the night of her murder. Whatever had happened, Catalina might hold the missing piece.

He drafted a message to Catalina, but something told him this wouldn't be a discussion she'd be open to easily. Those close to tragedy never wanted to talk, especially if they had something to hide. The visibility of the case guaranteed that people would be digging just to gather some shred of information concerning Lisa. Reaching out to her directly was unwise; certain journalists had already exploited the story, and vultures circled with their endless questions. Who could she trust? Who would she want to talk to under such scrutiny? Amore knew he would need a different approach.

He considered calling Greg; maybe to compare findings, maybe just to bounce ideas off someone who knew how to listen. But Greg hadn't been answering his calls. That silence nagged at him more than he wanted to admit.

Frustrated but determined not to be deterred, Amore went back to his notes. He was a seasoned journalist who had been down roads like this one before. The champagne, the drugs, the suite, the inconsistencies in Lisa's life.

Sitting by himself in his office, Amore tried to focus, but a name hung in the back of his mind like a thread of smoke: Lucius. The supposed journalist had appeared out of nowhere, dropping cryptic hints about Maxwell, then vanished just as quickly. Amore hadn't followed up, not yet. Something about Lucius made him hold back—not fear, exactly, but a deep-seated caution. He'd dealt with this type before: people who showed up bearing mystery wrapped in riddles, who told you just enough to keep you leaning forward but never quite enough to truly move you.

In his gut, Amore felt that subtle tightening of unease. Not quite unhinged, but a clear warning. A reminder. After everything he had endured for his search for truth—every betrayal, every attack—he had learned to be more cautious. He thought of all the wounds he was reopening by even thinking the name Maxwell again. The buried memories, the devastation that hadn't quite healed. It wasn't enough that he'd been ostracized by his colleagues, that half-whispers of his "bias" still drifted through every newsroom he dared walk into. It wasn't enough that his name—Amore Reyes—had once meant something and now mostly brought sidelong looks, polite nods, or worse, uncomfortable silence.

No, what tormented him most was the truth underlying it all. He'd flown too close to power. And like some poor bastard in a legend, his wings weren't forged of steel, but plastic. Thin. Flammable. Easily melted. He'd tried to hold Maxwell accountable, to pull on the strings of the man's empire, and in doing so, he'd given them every reason to label him compromised. Emotional. Vengeful. Unreliable.

Even now, he could still hear the tone in their voices: *You're too close to this, Amore. You've made it personal. That's not journal-ism. That's obsession.*

And maybe they were right. Maybe he had crossed a line. But he also knew what he had seen. What he had uncovered. What they chose to ignore.

Which made Lucius even more complicated.

Still… something about Lucius remained. Maybe it was his calm confidence. Maybe it was that he had mentioned Maxwell of his own accord. Or maybe it was just the fact that Lucius did not want anything, not yet. That made him either more dangerous—or more authentic. Amore could not tell. Was he genuine? A rogue journalist with real intel, someone who had gone off the grid and found something worth bringing back? Or was he just another opportunist—another person rummaging through the ruins of Amore's credibility, seeking to use him like others had? To feed him breadcrumbs. Watch him run. Then leave him holding the fallout.

All these questions spun in his mind, tangled together like static. And yet, despite the caution, despite the scars, something deeper stirred: Curiosity. The same thing that had ruined him once—and made him what he was. Maybe there was something here. Something he missed. Something he hadn't connected yet. A loose thread that Lucius could pull on just enough to unravel the next layer. Maybe the man's sudden appearance wasn't chance.

But he knew: Lucius wasn't going anywhere. He was just… waiting. Out there in the periphery somewhere. Because if Lucius had something concrete—anything concrete—Amore wasn't going to let it slip through the cracks. Not this time.

For now, Amore returned his attention to the case in front of him. Lisa. Catalina. The champagne. The suite. All of it tangled up in inconsistencies.

Chapter 9

The Art of the Approach

When investigating a story, two things are essential to validating the truth: sources and facts.

You can have a source that sounds credible, maybe even sound trustworthy. But if the facts aren't there, the story collapses under the weight of speculation. This is the trap most beginning journalists fall into. They go after what sounds good. They believe what they want to believe. But real journalism? That is all about balance. Delicate, deliberate balance.

You have to ask yourself, why is this person telling me this? Are they trying to help? To protect themselves? Are they giving me truth, half-truths, or the version that makes them look the best? What do they gain? What do they lose by telling me?

Questions about Catalina Gomez were present. She was a mystery wrapped in social awareness, always just close enough to what was happening, but never quite fully in the spotlight. She appeared in the background of the nightclub video with Lisa, holding a champagne bottle, yelling out into the night as if she owned it. But that was just one image, one moment of a larger story. The rest of her online presence was carefully curated and, in some cases, almost surgically modified to maintain what she wanted the public to know.

What Amore had managed to piece together so far was circumstantial at best: Catalina and Lisa had known each other for years, through parties, tagged photos, birthdays, and shared networking events. Lisa had been the wide-eyed intern still trying to find her place. Catalina had already established herself in the vast world of media. She worked for a different media company, and while her role didn't directly overlap with Lisa's, Amore's pulse quickened when he traced the company's parent conglomerate: **Piermont**. The name hit him like a physical blow, a ghost from his past. It was the same media titan he'd tried to expose during his Maxwell investigation, a name he'd never expected to see again. Back then, every door had been sealed, every lead blocked. Seeing it now meant this wasn't just another case—it was a second chance.

Catalina was an integral part of learning more about Lisa. The various gaps he had uncovered so far were only surface level. What he wanted was a sense of who she truly was—not just a victim, but the actual person. From the brief photos he had seen, it was clear there was a bond between Lisa and Catalina. That bond could shed light on who Lisa was outside of her checkered life.

The issue that lingered was how to reach Catalina, and whether she would even be willing to speak with him. But all that would be for nothing if he couldn't gain her trust. Amore knew better than to come at her directly. Not with an accusation. Especially not after all that she'd just lost a close friend in the most public, heartbreaking way. If he went at her as a journalist hungry for the next scoop, she would shut him down. Or worse—refer him to the authorities. He could not risk making another misstep.

He started with her routine: observation. He had to find the opening and approach her with care. Ruling out abrasive phone calls wasn't an option—they wouldn't come off as genuine. Surprising her at her home was the next thing off the table. Risky as it was, he had to find an opening that suited her comfort. Studying her patterns, the best angle seemed to be through her job. It was a delicate approach, bordering on an intrusion into her private life, but he couldn't see another way. He would have to watch and wait for the right moment. Catalina made it slightly easier: she lived by her routines. Around lunchtime, she typically slipped away, always at the same time, always by herself. It was an opening.

She had lunch at a small café at 8th and Wells, tucked into the rear street of a media complex. It was quiet, with minimal foot traffic. She always ordered the same thing: a latte and a chocolate chip bagel, with a side of cream cheese. She'd take a seat in the rear, make a call or scroll her phone, eat quickly, and leave. She was there two to four days per week, always alone and always on the phone.

On the fourth day, he saw her again. Same routine. She was at the counter, earbuds in, softly laughing at something on her phone. It wasn't the ideal time to talk, but his options were limited. This was a calculated risk.

He approached the counter, stepping in line just behind her. She was on her phone, lost in her own world, her earbuds in. As she reached to grab her latte, Amore took a deep breath. "Catalina?" he said softly, his voice low enough not to startle her but clear enough to cut through the cafe's chatter.

Her eyes sharpened. She pulled out one of her earbuds, arms folding over her chest, her stance shifting rapidly from relaxed too defensive. "Do I know you?"

"No," Amore said. "My name is Amore. I was hoping to talk. It's about Lisa."

Her expression darkened instantly. She stepped back slightly. "Are you serious right now? This is on my lunch break, at my job. I'm going to call the police if you do not get the hell out of my space."

"I know this comes out of the blue," he said, hands up a bit, palms out. "And I'm sorry to interrupt you like this—but I've been attempting to find out more about her. Not what's happened to her—about who she was. And your name was mentioned."

"I don't care," she snapped, a flash of emotion in her eyes. "You think because someone dies, you can go around intruding on their lives like they're specimens. She was my friend—not your story."

"I understand that. I do. This is not ideal for me as well," Amore said, softening his voice. "I'm not here searching for the next headline or with a film crew. I'm not trying to sensationalize anything. I just… I think people should remember Lisa for more than where she died. Like you said, she was a person with a life of her own."

Catalina's teeth gritted. "You have no idea what kind of pain this has caused me. What type of people have shown up at my job. Messaged me on DMs. Journalists like yourself. Even police officers questioning me as if I did something wrong. And you want to talk? What makes you any different from the rest?"

"I'm not trying to add to that," he said, his tone calm, steady. "I just want to understand who she was. And I thought maybe you'd want someone to actually listen, not just pump you for details."

She looked at him for what felt like an eternity—her eyes flashing as if she was measuring every word, every inch of him. Then, finally, her shoulders dropped just slightly.

"You're not taping this, are you?"

"No," he said. "No microphone. No recorder. Just coffee and a conversation—if you're up to it."

Her eyes welled up, but she blinked the tears back before they fell. "You want to hear about Lisa?"

"I do. And not just what went down at the hotel. I want to know her life. Who she was to the people who really knew her."

Catalina exhaled, the tension in her jaw slowly easing. "If that's really your take, and this is not another spin piece, then perhaps we can talk."

"I promise," he said, turning to her. "I'm not here for a story. I just want the truth."

She paused, turning to him again. Then nodded ever so slightly.

"But not here," she said quietly. "I do not want anyone at my job to think that I have something else going on. They've already got me on a short leash."

"I understand," Amore said. "Completely."

She pulled out her phone. "I'll text you a place. Somewhere discreet. Tonight."

"Thanks," he said sincerely.

Catalina threw him one final look. "Don't make me regret this. I'm not a source for your story. Lisa was more than what happened to her. And if I think for one second, you're twisting my words, I promise you, you will regret it."

"Got it."

And then she disappeared—bagel clutched in hand, latte in the other, earbuds back in, but the armor just a little less rigid.

Chapter 10

The Party and the Players

A light drizzle swept through the night. The weather felt almost fitting for meeting Catalina, who was particular about the meeting setting. It was as if she had taken notes from the Secret Service, carefully choosing a spot in the heart of downtown. The place she picked was quaint yet lively, a social hub designed to foster interaction, relaxation, and entertainment. Unlike a quiet coffee shop or low-key bar, this lounge mirrored her personality: defined by high energy and a constant flow of social engagement.

Amore stepped through the entrance, his coat still damp from the light rain. His eyes, calm and experienced, swept the room; he was a man accustomed to walking into uncomfortable spaces. Inside, the establishment buzzed with life. People of all ages filled the space, moving to the rhythm of a DJ spinning from the stage. Warm, strategic lighting bathed the room in an intimate glow, shaping the atmosphere into something both electric and inviting. He spotted Catalina tucked into a reserved corner, in a tight booth. Her shoulders were curled, tense under a mini jacket. Despite the commotion, Catalina remained composed, a figure separated in her own world, waiting for his arrival. She was scrolling through her phone, not really looking at anything, her eyes flashing up every now and then as he approached. Her face was a mask of practiced calm, a blank expression betraying only a hint of doubt. Though bathed in light, she wore sunglasses perched on her head, and her eyes, when they finally met his, carried the weight of someone trying to avoid truths.

He slid into the seat across from her. "I didn't think you'd show," he said quietly.

Catalina didn't answer right away. She reached for the drink in front of her, swirling it, watching the ice rise to the top. "I almost didn't," she said finally, her voice low. She met his gaze. "You're asking questions no one else is. That makes me nervous."

Amore leaned forward, his elbows on the table. "I'm not here for a story. I'm here because Lisa mattered. There was more to her than what's printed."

Catalina laughed, a short, sharp sound. "Oh sure. You're one of the good ones. A conscience-stricken reporter. Where were you when she died?"

He didn't flinch. "Covering another story. But now I'm here."

She fixed her gaze on him, her eyes sharp and unyielding, as if looking straight through him. Her voice was a blend of cynicism and curiosity. "So, let me ask you this—what makes Lisa so special to you? Why are you going out of your way for a woman you barely knew? Everyone else is drawn to her because she's a dead woman in a hotel—nothing more, nothing less. I've seen journalists chase stories they don't truly understand. So tell me… why do you want to know about Lisa?"

Her questions cut deep. He couldn't form an honest answer. In truth, the thought that she might have been murdered—and that someone needed to be held accountable—was his first instinct. But saying that out loud felt shallow, like another reporter's line for sympathy. Without thinking, he fell back on the memory of what had first drawn him in.

"I looked at photos of Lisa," he said quietly. "What captivated me most wasn't her death, but her energy—her lease on life. It's one thing to write about a person based only on reports, reducing them to a headline. But you knew her. You experienced the moments I never could. So… tell me. What was she really like to you?"

"You two were close, huh?" Amore began, feeling his way around the edge of something.

Catalina hesitated, nodding just a little. "Lisa and I met at a corporate function about two years ago. We both hated it, so we skipped out early and wound up getting tacos from a food truck. That night we talked more than I've talked to some members of my own family."

He leaned forward. "So you stayed close?"

"Yeah. She was the kind of person who made you feel like she was all-in even with a dozen things going on simultaneously. Her calendar intimidated me just by hearing about it. But somehow, she never failed to make time." Catalina smiled faintly. "She was more present than anyone I've ever met."

"What was she working on recently?"

Catalina's expression flickered. "Influencer arrangements, content scheduling, that sort of thing. But that's not what kept her up at night. Lately… she was pursuing something. Something bigger. She wouldn't say what, exactly, but I could tell."

Amore cocked his head to one side. "What do you mean?"

She stared at him for a long moment. Her body language shifted defensively, but there was something else in her eyes: exhaustion, maybe, or regret.

"She was… luminous," Catalina broke her silence, her words dropping to a whisper. "Adventurous. If you had ever met her, she would have left a mark on you. She knew how to move in rooms most people couldn't walk into without choking. But she had these… moods. Spells of silence. Like she wanted to disappear from all of it. And the more intense her work got, the harder those spells came."

Amore listened in silence.

"Mingling with high-end people was her norm. Dated some genuine pieces of shit, too. But she never let anyone in too deep. Not even me."

He spoke hesitantly. "What about the champagne?"

Catalina stiffened. Her hand froze in mid-sip. Her expression didn't just shift; her energy did. "What?"

"The champagne bottle. It was found in her suite. It stood out."

"What does that have to do with me?" Catalina rebuked.

"It doesn't have anything to do with you," Amore replied evenly. "But there was a video online showing you and Lisa with that same bottle the night before her death."

She slapped the glass down. "You stalking me now? Digging through pictures like some crazy creep?"

"I've been looking into Lisa," he corrected her. "You just happened to be someone she trusted. Not a crime. I saw something that didn't make sense. It wasn't about you—it was about her. That bottle was placed there. Or at least, it was significant. I'm not accusing. I'm just trying to figure it out."

"No. We're finished." She stood up, reaching for her purse. "I shouldn't have come here. I knew this was a bad idea." She began to walk away, but stopped as Amore called, his voice a calm and measured counterpoint to her rage. It was low enough to be heavy with authenticity, and it stopped her cold.

She stood there, torn between flight and fight.

"This isn't about you. It's about her. Lisa doesn't get to speak for herself anymore. But that doesn't mean her story doesn't get told."

"You think I don't still hold that night with me?" she let out a low screamed, her voice cracking. "You think I don't replay it in my head, question myself for not going upstairs after her, for not yanking her back, stopping her from—" She cut herself off, her eyes welling with tears.

He stood there, not pursuing her, but standing in solidarity. "You couldn't have known. But you know more than anyone who has talked to me. And if something happened that night—something that was covered up—don't you want to be certain it doesn't happen again?"

A long pause. Her shoulders relaxed, just slightly.

"Okay," she gasped. "I'll tell you what I remember. But don't quote me. Don't name me. Don't even imply I said anything to you."

Amore nodded once.

"Sit down," she told him.

They returned to the booth, and Catalina sat down again, slowly this time. She didn't look at him as she began to speak.

"Lisa was dealing with something bigger than a party. Something bigger than that room. I didn't understand it, and I don't think she did either. But she was scared. Joking about it, brushing it off—but underneath, I could tell. She wasn't okay."

"That night… Lisa didn't even want to go. The party was being sponsored by **NDX Group**—they're one of the subsidiaries of **Veritas Dominion**, a media company so damn big it has companies within companies. Lisa's company was partnered with them somehow. I don't even know how deep it went."

Amore didn't take notes; he merely listened.

"It wasn't a public event. It was a private gathering. Top executives, celebrities, politicians. Name them, they were there. Even **Gargon Maxwell** made an appearance."

Amore's jaw tightened and went still. The name hit like a punch to the gut. His heart thumped, just once, too loud in his chest. But his face didn't shift. He took a sip of the water he had ordered instead of the whiskey. Catalina was already staring at him more intensely. She tilted her head. "You know him?"

"I know of him," Amore said. "It's impossible not to."

She didn't press, but she had picked up on his subtle shift. A held breath that lasted too long. A blink that came a little too slowly.

Catalina's gaze wandered beyond Amore, landing somewhere among the faces in the lounge. Her fingers traced the rim of her glass as if the movement might summon courage. "She trusted him more than the others," she said eventually. "At least… she believed so."

Amore said nothing. He could sense the weight behind the restraint in her words.

"Dax Duvall," she murmured. "The radio personality. Syndicated. Boisterous. Flashy. Always talking like he's got the world figured out, like every moment's a performance."

Amore raised an eyebrow. "The morning show host?"

Catalina gave a short, humorless laugh. "Yeah. That one. He was the one who invited her to the party. Big VIP energy, knew all the back doors. She brought me in at the last minute." Her voice fell. "She told me it was for work, but something didn't feel right."

"She had been working on some kind of 'project.' She never gave details, just little sighs and complaints. Whatever it was, it was pissing her off. But she played the game. Lisa always did."

Catalina looked down at her drink.

Amore leaned forward slightly. "Who else was there?"

Catalina shifted restlessly, her eyes intensifying. "I shouldn't — look, this isn't easy to talk about. Let's just say this: I didn't know half of the people. But I recognized a few." She paused. "Victor Haines. You know him?"

"Political analyst. Network guy," Amore quipped. "Claims to be neutral but doesn't shut up about preserving the political status quo."

Catalina nodded. "That's him. Slicker than grease, like he can sell you your own eviction notice. Always around the power players, always smiling like he knows something the rest of us don't."

She hesitated, then went on: "He was close to someone that night. Don't know if it was business or something else."

Amore let that hang.

"There was another one—Jett Carson. Sports media. Boisterous. Argues for a living. I think he got into it with someone near the bar. Has to be the loudest voice in the room, whether anyone is listening or not."

Amore smirked. "Controversy pays his bills."

"And the kid… younger than the others. **Flex**. The streamer. Millions of views. I had no idea who he was until Lisa showed him to me. He was trying to live stream parts of the evening when he got here. All jokes and hype until someone told him to put the phone away. Then he went upstairs and disappeared."

Amore's eyes narrowed. "Was Lisa with him?"

Catalina paused. "She was around them. All of them. But mainly… she was tense. Preoccupied. Like she was trying to convince herself she was having a good time."

"Did she say why?"

Catalina shook her head. "She mentioned something about a conversation she needed to have— 'big picture' stuff, whatever that means. She wasn't thrilled but she downplayed it. And when she did finally pull away to 'mingle,' that was the last I saw of her."

"We had champagne delivered in advance. She organized everything. We were partying like we didn't have a care in the world. Pills, drinks, the entire rockstar lifestyle." Her voice cracked, just barely. "She told me she was going to talk to someone about her future plans. Then she smiled and said to go ahead and enjoy myself, it's a party. Next thing I know… she's got Dax, Jett, and Flex hovering around her. Then off they went to the VIP room."

"She was still clutching the bottle. I saw it. That's the last time I saw her alive."

She didn't speak another word for what felt like an eternity, choosing her words carefully.

"And Dax—the man she came with?" Amore asked.

She turned away, eyes unyielding. "I haven't seen him since. Not on air, not online. As if he took a break after it happened."

Amore's tone altered—low and resolute. "You've given me more than you know. And I give you my word, if there is truth to be found in this… I'll find it."

Catalina exhaled, releasing something heavy. She rose then, grabbing her bag with care. "I should go. I wasn't even supposed to talk about this with anyone."

Amore stood with her. "Why did you?"

"I don't know. Maybe it's some strange survivor's guilt, and I needed to clear my conscience. Or maybe I just wanted to talk to someone."

Catalina began walking to the exit, this time more resolute. "If you need anything else, reach out. Just don't expect me to do this twice."

She gave him one last look—both fragile and fierce—before turning and disappearing into the crowd.

Amore lingered in the booth alone, her words echoing inside him. He signaled the bartender.

"Another?" the man asked.

"Yeah," Amore spoke quietly. "Make it a strong one."

He didn't know what exactly he had just walked into. But it was bigger than even Lisa's death. It was Veritas Dominion.

Chapter 11

Endgame

BANG! BANG! BANG!

The ringing metal echoed across the porch and down the empty street, a hammer against the stillness. A porch light flickered on, illuminating the brick steps and doorway with a bright glow. Inside, slow, shuffling footsteps approached.

"Who is it? What do you want?" a growling voice demanded from behind the door.

Amore pushed forward. "It's me. Amore. Open the door."

The deadbolt slid. The door creaked open, and Greg's face emerged. He was wearing a wrinkled T-shirt and basketball shorts, his expression tense and disheveled.

"Amore…? Are you kidding me right now?" Greg snapped. "It's the middle of the night. Why the hell are you knocking on my door like the Damm police? I'm trying to have some peace and quiet."

Amore waved his hand, his voice firm but urgent. "I know, I know. Sorry for just dropping by, but it's important." He glanced toward the empty driveway. "Elaine and the kids are out. You're alone."

Greg's gaze narrowed to a thin squint. "Whether they're here or not is irrelevant. I said I wanted some quiet time."

"Another way of saying you've been avoiding me," Amore said icily. "I've called. Sent texts. Nothing. So yeah—this was the best I could manage."

"I'm not avoiding you," Greg grumbled, stepping back unwillingly to let him in. "I've just had a lot on my plate. What's so pressing you had to come by now?"

Amore entered the living room, which was dim except for the low glow of a TV. He paced once, then stopped. Greg stood facing him, arms crossed, rubbing his temples. He made no move to sit.

"Alright. What is it?" Greg asked, his voice laced with annoyance. "You haven't seen me since the park, and now you're here."

"I met someone—Catalina," Amore said, his hands moving restlessly as he spoke, as if still unraveling the details in his mind. "Lisa's friend. The girl she invited to the party that night. I was able to track her down, and it turns out she was her closest friend. There's more to all of this, Greg. A lot more."

Greg's eyes went cold. "Lisa? The girl I talked about a few weeks ago—the suicide victim? You're coming to me in headlines. What are you really saying?"

Amore leaned in, took a deep breath, and lowered his tone. "Lisa didn't go to that party for fun. She was dating Dax Duvall, allegedly. He's the one who invited her, and Catalina said Lisa didn't want to go at first. But he insisted."

Greg raised a skeptical brow. "You're telling me Lisa was dating the loudmouthed radio clown?"

"I didn't believe it either," Amore admitted. "But that's not the point. It's who else was there. Victor Haines. Jett Carson. Even—Flex."

"The streamer?" Greg laughed dryly. "What, was this some kind of influencer party?"

"They're all tied to something way bigger than we can grasp right now. And I've seen pieces of it before from past work. Not to mention Maxwell was there as well, which only heightens my suspicion."

Greg waited, and then—"Maxwell."

Greg leaned back and exhaled a sharp breath through his nose. He stared at Amore, unblinking. "Do you hear yourself right now?"

"I know how it sounds—"

"No, you don't," Greg interrupted. "Because if you did, you wouldn't be standing in my living room in the middle of the night telling me about Maxwell."

"I am not guessing," Amore snapped. "I am going where the story takes me. Real leads. Catalina shared things that correlate. The bottle of champagne Lisa brought wasn't random. And all of them—Duvall, Haines, Carson, Flex—they all connect to Veritas Dominion."

Greg stood up. "You're spiraling. You're dragging a dead woman's name through conspiracy theories based on vague party stories."

"That's not right," Amore said, his voice deepening.

"What's not right is you barging into my home without a shred of evidence. No footage, no texts, no records? No coroner's dispute, no suspicious autopsy?"

Amore's hands clenched at his sides. He didn't have solid evidence—not yet. But his bones were screaming he was close. "I just wanted to tell you what I've learned. She said Maxwell was there."

"And?" asked Greg. "You still don't know what that means. Or if it even matters. Maybe he was. It's a party. Rich people circulate."

Amore's voice rose, every word striking at Greg. "You forget—it was you who came to me about a dead girl. You asked me to look into it, for the sake of her family. And I did. Now, suddenly, I need your help and you're nowhere to be found. You sent me down this path, and now all you can do is tell me I'm losing it? Do you even hear yourself? I'm drowning in this, and all you do is watch."

The room went still. Greg's face twisted anger mixed with disappointment, and underneath it, hurt.

"Yeah, I pushed you toward it," Greg shot back. "But look at you now. You're not thinking straight. You don't listen—you bend everything to your own convictions, like the world always must line up with how you see it. You're making me the bad guy so you can keep chasing this. I'm not abandoning you, but as a journalist you know this has no merit. If I published what you're saying, it would read like a hit piece—and everything would come crashing down. But you don't see that, because in your mind, you're always right."

"I'm not trying to pull you in," Amore said. "But I thought if anyone would at least listen—"

"I am listening," Greg cut in, his voice firm. "And I'm telling you this as someone who gives a crap. You'd best get a grip. Whatever you're chasing, just ensure it doesn't kill you in the process."

The air thickened. Greg tilted his head, skeptical. "You're telling me the only thing connecting any of this is a champagne bottle and a secondhand conversation with a woman you barely know?"

"I don't have all my facts yet—"

"Because you don't have any," Greg cut in. "You have circumstance. Circumstance doesn't fly. And even if—if—there's something to this, where is it leading? What's the endgame here?"

Amore didn't respond.

Greg stepped forward. "Is this to prove it wasn't an overdose? Because from where I'm standing, it looks like you're chasing nothing. Maybe for justice, maybe for guilt, but this is sounding increasingly like validation for yourself. Like if you expose something, then you get to feel whole again. But what is this really about? If it's a murder conspiracy, a cover-up involving media personalities, do you know what that is?"

"I do," Amore muttered.

"No," Greg said, softer. "I don't think you do. Because if you did, you'd be scared. You'd be careful. Not bursting through my door with nothing but instinct and a champagne bottle."

There was silence. The TV flickered.

Then Amore said, slowly, "You've known me for years, Greg. You think I'd gamble everything on a whim? I don't know what this is yet, but it's pulling at something within me. Something I hadn't felt in a long time. And if there's even a chance that it's true—that Lisa came too close to something she wasn't supposed to understand—then I need to know. I don't give a damn about the politics or the noise. But Maxwell was there. Catalina said so. That name is significant. You know that as well as I do."

Greg looked away for a moment, his tone lowering when he continued. "You're not thinking. You're running headlong into something with teeth, and you don't even see it yet. Maxwell's not a byline. He's got corporate hands in the media. Real ones. We've been down this path; it's how you got where you are. If his name's tied to any of this—even slightly—then you're compromised just by proximity."

Amore's throat tightened.

Greg stepped closer, leveling with him. "You could lose everything. Your credibility. Your safety. You're a journalist, Amore—but you're acting like an idealist. And idealists don't survive people like Maxwell."

For a long moment, Amore said nothing. His gaze dropped. Greg's words weren't wrong. They stung precisely because they weren't.

Finally, Amore whispered, almost to himself, "If you're not here to help me… then I'll do it by myself."

Greg's face flashed with pain, maybe regret. Amore walked toward the door.

"I get it now," he said. "You're avoiding me because you think I'm reckless. A liability. Someone who can drag your name down too. I'm not stupid. I'll figure it out on my own."

He placed his hand on the doorknob.

Greg's voice behind him. "Wait."

Amore turned halfway. "If you'd like my help, I'll give it to you," Greg said. "But you need to come with concrete evidence. I mean hard stuff. Documents. Records. A timeline. Give me something I can cross-reference. Something I can show to people who matter." He stepped closer. "Otherwise… you're not chasing truth. You're chasing closure. And that's not journalism. That's just therapy with a trail of collateral damage."

Amore glared at him, conflicted.

"I'll do what's best for the story," Amore said quietly. "But I'll also do what's right for Lisa."

Amore pulled the door open, stepping out into the quiet night. The confrontation with Greg stung, but it only solidified his resolve.

Chapter 12

Inevitable Encounter

Greg's voice lingered in Amore's head long after the door had closed. His words—"You don't have hard evidence. You're spiraling."—rang like a guilty verdict, a truth too sharp to ignore. He lay back on his living room couch, staring aimlessly at the ceiling, his laptop resting on the coffee table. He hadn't even kicked off his shoes. The cheap fan above spun in slow rotations that matched the drift of his thoughts. He had no evidence. He had no witness. Greg wasn't delusional.

All he had was a feeling. A cold, persistent weight in his gut that told him Lisa's death was not just another senseless overdose. That feeling had led him to groundbreaking stories before, stories that had made him a name at *The Inquisitor*. But that was then, and this was now. **Beyond Reach** was in its infancy, just starting to get traction from the public—a machine that barely worked, held together by people whose only goal was to shed light on topics that matter. If he pushed this story and got it wrong—even slightly—it wouldn't just destroy him; it would bring down the entire operation. All the writers he had hired would pay the price for his gamble.

He sighed, rubbing the bridge of his nose. He could just walk away from it all, leak the details anonymously, and let someone else fight for a half-baked story. But they wouldn't see Lisa. They would see content in the form of a quick headline, not caring about the human aspect behind it. All it would read is a young girl who partied too hard and did it to herself. That wasn't what Catalina told him. His conviction pressed hard against his soul. Catalina had trusted him with the small piece of information she was willing to share, and to twist that trust for his own doubts would be to betray her.

The thought gnawed at him, a reminder that the line between persistence and violation was thinner than he wanted to admit.

If Lisa didn't overdose… if she was made to look like she did—why? What did she know? Who did she threaten? He had no credentials, clearance, or connections without some form of corruption. Greg was out. He would not provide access, not like this. And even if he did, the trail would always lead back to **Beyond Reach**. That couldn't happen.

He sat up and reached for his laptop. Naima's name sat at the top of his chat thread.

AMORE: Need a favor. Quick cross-check. Look up any historic tie-ins between Newtech Industries and Veritas Dominion. Anything that connects them—partnerships, mergers, think tanks, joint projects. Could be buried.

Her response came faster than he expected.

NAIMA: Already on it. Give me 10.

Amore leaned forward, his legs bouncing. He opened a secondary folder of clippings—old cases, archived notes from his final months at *The Inquisitor*. He remembered writing these vaguely. At the time, they were corporate intrigue dressed up as news, and he'd never have thought they would intersect. A message beeped. Naima again.

NAIMA: There is a connection. A quiet one. **Veritas Dominion** created a private merger with a venture funded by **Newtech** three years ago. No public press announcement. I had to pull the information from leaked investor briefings. The merger provided Dominion with entertainment consumer data. In return, Newtech got proprietary influence over Dominion's algorithm development. It was marketed internally as "strategic media synthesis." Sound familiar?

Amore sat back on his couch, stunned for a moment. He opened the news briefing Naima sent. There it was; **NewTech Synthesis,** a shell firm set up as an intermediary. No logo. No board members. Just a PO box in Delaware and a paper trail of jargon. He clicked back to one of his older pieces—an exposé on corporate surveillance. A couple of the anonymous sources, their names blurred then, lined up with the people Catalina had mentioned.

His gaze narrowed. He'd only scratched the surface back then. Now that same surface was cracking. Still…it was all circumstantial. Not close to being publishable. But there were cracks. And cracks let in light.

He slumped back, his mind racing. He needed more information. Greg was out. He sorted through names in his mind like an old Rolodex. Former sources. Contacts. Reporters. No one worked. Then he stopped. **Lucius**.

The name simply sat there. A hint of something that hadn't yet taken form. He didn't trust him—not at all. But Lucius had shown up in his office with leads and a gaze that suggested he was already a few steps ahead.

He reached for the business card. Held it between his fingers. Thick cardstock. Letters pressed into the surface that sank into the paper like scars. Could he trust this man? Did he have any choice?

"To hell with it," he muttered, grabbing his phone and dialing the number.

The phone rang once. Twice. Three times. Nothing. He set it down, ready to write it off, when it vibrated. The light on the screen flashed. Lucius.

He picked it up. "Lucius?"

There was a pause.

"Yeah," Lucius said, his voice rough and half-muffled through static. "I'm here. Took you long enough to call."

"Timing's everything," Amore replied.

A beat went by. Silence. Then the gentle shuffling of papers.

"You're not calling me just to talk," Lucius stated. "So what changed?"

"Curiosity," Amore replied. "You dropped a name I haven't heard in a while. Got me wondering how you came across it."

"You mean Maxwell," Lucius said, clearly amused. "Didn't think a name that big would come from someone like me?"

"Something like that. You came at an interesting time, said interesting things. Just trying to figure out if you're actually in the conversation or if you're just repeating headlines."

Lucius hesitated, then his tone turned softer—almost playful. "You want to know how deep the Maxwell connection goes."

Amore didn't take the bait. "I want to know why you brought him up. You came to my office, remember?"

"Look," Amore said, cutting to the chase. "If this is just another dead-end with a guy trying to leverage scraps into relevance, I don't have time. But—if there is something you actually know, something worth looking into… I'm listening."

"Now we're getting somewhere," Lucius said. "But hearing and listening are two different things."

"Then give me something worth hearing."

Another silence. This one lasted longer. Amore swore he could hear Lucius's grin.

Lucius broke his silence. "We can talk. When you're ready. But I'm not going to share information over the phone."

Amore frowned. "You approached me. You made yourself available. If you had something—just enough to make this believable—you'd share it. So what's your play here?"

Lucius smiled softly. "You don't trust me. That's fair. I wouldn't trust me either. But you called because you wanted to. You're desperate for a lead, and you know this is a viable path."

Still, Amore kept his tone flat. "You mentioned meeting in person. Still on the table?"

"Only if you're going to stop pretending, you're just curious."

"You're the one who called," Amore smiled thinly. "Perhaps I'm just being polite."

Lucius kept the silence going a beat longer. Then: "Fine. I'll give you the address of a place I know. Quiet. Neutral. Tomorrow. 1 p.m."

Amore hesitated.

"One condition," Lucius interrupted. "You come alone."

"Fine," Amore muttered. "But if I show up and you waste my time—"

"You'll walk. I get it. But you won't."

"Good. I'll be there." The phone went dead.

Amore stared at the screen, thoughtful. The message arrived seconds later.

A coffee shop on the city's east side. Simple. Off the radar. If Lucius was playing a bluff, he was pulling it off masterfully. If not, then he might be the only one who could help him fit the pieces together.

Chapter 13

The Voice in the Static

The crisp morning sky swept across the city buildings. Daylight was soon arriving, pushing back the lingering darkness. At this hour, countless people were still swallowed by their beds, trying to steal a little more sleep before the day began—but not Amore. This was his time for clarity. Dressed in a gray and white sweatsuit, he savored the quiet moment, taking a jog before the day truly started. The pavement hit back with each stride, rhythmic and even, as though trying to remind Amore that he was quite alive. His breathing was measured, even—years of running had made this more than a ritual. It was comfort. He ran the deserted streets before the city awoke. Cool air closed around him, biting but fleeting, the kind that brings on a memory.

It wasn't about movement. It was about repetition. Predictability. Step after step, forward momentum when every-thing else around him felt like fragments of unfinished stories. He wasn't sure whether he was chasing clarity or running away from the confused chaos of it all. Maybe both. Maybe neither. Each time he'd gotten close to something enormous, he was here—sweating, alone, moving forward. The cadence of his sneakers on the ground sounded almost prophetic.

He veered toward the old side of the park, where fewer people ran and the trail twisted more like thought. That's where she came to him—Melanie. Not in person, but in the way memories do when they know you're vulnerable. He could still see her sitting on the edge of their bed, wrapped in sunlight and skepticism, teasing him for being too absorbed in a concept, too lost in the thrill of the unraveling. He turned with his back to home, firm in heart now, and not in mind. He thought of Maxwell, the empire of silence he built. He thought of Dominion, how corruption came dressed as a smile. And then Lisa.

And he stopped. Halted. Lisa. She had been only a name. Another tragic line in a police report. But something about her refused to leave him alone. He'd seen others die before. Innocents lost. Names smudged in ink. But this one—this case clung to him like smoke. Why? He didn't know her. She meant nothing to him. But yet—she meant everything. Was it Maxwell? The silence that clung to her? Or was it something greater? This case felt like a personal challenge, a relentless pull demanding answers.

Resuming his jog, Amore pushed his thoughts back and focused on what lay ahead—the meeting with Lucius and whatever it might bring. From behind, he caught the rapid beat of approaching footsteps. He thought little of it—probably just another runner. Shifting closer to the edge of the trail, he gave space to pass. The steps grew louder. Closer. Closer.

Then, out of nowhere, their bodies collided. Amore hit the ground with a heavy thud while the stranger remained standing. Grass stains smeared across his sweatsuit as he groaned, clutching his shoulder. Pain throbbed sharply as he looked up at the man towering over him, face unreadable.

"What the fuck?!" Amore shouted. "I gave you room to pass, and you still ran into me!"

The man studied him with a cold, taunting calm. "Your eyes weren't focused. You need to get your head together." Then he broke into a run again, each stride carrying him further down the trail. Just before he vanished into the distance, his voice drifted back:

"Be more careful, Amore."

Amore froze. His name. *How the hell did he know my name?*

Grimacing, he pushed himself up, brushing off dirt with disbelief as the ache in his shoulder deepened.

The pain in his shoulder was still a dull throb as Amore approached Teller's later that afternoon. He was twenty minutes early, as promised—an old habit, a way of keeping control. The coffee shop, Teller's, was buried on a side road in Ashridge Park, behind a faded, tattered bookstore and an overgrown ivy wall. Outside, it appeared to have been abandoned by time—wood trim, chalkboards listing specials, a bell that rang as the door swung open.

He lingered outside the door, silently glancing through the glass to survey the inside. His intent was simple: get a read on Lucius before the man could catch sight of him. Any cue—posture, body language, energy. Anything to make this feel less like walking blind into a setup.

But by the time he entered, Lucius was waiting.

Front corner booth. Back to the window. Facing the door.

Waiting.

It startled him more than he wanted to admit.

Lucius sat with a calmness that felt calculated. He stirred his tea slowly, as if time was at his beck and call. His jacket was draped on the chair beside him, collar slightly turned up. Nothing flashy. Nothing too clean. But there was a sharp edge hidden beneath, like armor hidden under cotton and charm. His presence was controlled, measured. A man you'd notice from across the room, then forget until it was too late. He looked centered, like someone who had walked through chaos and made peace with it.

His eyes met Amore's before he even fully crossed the room. A flicker of recognition—not surprise, not pleasure. Just acknowledgment.

Amore adjusted his jacket and approached, every step feeling more deliberate than he intended. Like a deer catching a glint of something just beyond the trees. Still, he walked toward it.

Lucius looked up, his face calm and unreadable, offering a nod. "You're early."

"You're earlier," Amore replied, forcing ease into his voice as he sat.

Lucius smiled faintly and put his spoon precisely beside the cup. "Always am. It helps to know how people move when they think no one's watching."

Amore leaned back, observing him now that he was closer. The man was as opposite as could be—laid-back in demeanor, yet intensely aware. Not an ounce of wasted motion. No phone on the table. No computer. Only tea. And the kind of gaze that could see past you if you weren't careful.

"So," Amore began tentatively, "Teller's, huh?"

"Best tea this side of town," Lucius stated, then added, "Also the kind of place people could forget the minute they leave."

Amore didn't smile.

Lucius's eyes lingered on him for a moment, sharp but not aggressive. "Thank you for coming. It's… fascinating, really. Seeing you in person again."

Amore raised an eyebrow. "Do you really follow my work?"

Lucius stirred his tea, one slow rotation of the spoon before putting it to the side of the cup. "Closely. For years. What you have done on **Beyond Reach**—the exposés, the danger… it's the type of journalism that makes us other writers question why we did not do this instead. Your instincts have eclipsed what I've spent most of my career chasing."

Amore leaned back, wary of the compliments. "Careful. You're making it sound like I have any clue what I'm doing."

Lucius smiled fleetingly. "That's what makes it so brilliant. You do— and you don't. That's what makes your work unique."

Amore's tone hardened. "Then tell me. What drew you to Maxwell? Most people run from a story like his. You ran toward it."

Lucius tilted his head slightly, but said nothing.

Amore pressed, his voice low. "You're not mentioned in any of the pieces I have found. No bylines. No interviews. It's like you have ghosted your entire career. So, how does a man with no name suddenly surface in the orbit of one of the most powerful men in data manipulation?"

Lucius set his cup down with a gentle tap. "I could ask you the same. The Times, the Post, even the London World Tribune; all dragged your name through the mud because of the reach of one man. The same man." His gaze narrowed. "That's why I was drawn to you. Because if someone's willing to sacrifice their life for the truth, it generally means they've got the potential to destroy the lie being told."

Amore did not blink. "You still haven't answered my question." He leaned in. "How did you come across Maxwell? What were your motives? And do not play games with me. Give me details. Make me believe you have something to offer."

Lucius's expression altered. Less charm. More calculation. A man weighing whether or not to pull back the curtain.

"Very well," he said, folding his hands neatly in front of him. "It started out as a routine investigation. A small piece—one of dozens I had written under the radar. It involved a cluster of companies connected to **NewTech**, mostly through shell organizations. One had a new platform—**PostHub**—rolled out with much hype and minimal regulation. I started to notice unusual spikes in data activity, particularly around user behavior models and unauthorized access logs."

He paused, eyes distant for a moment. "Then I learned about a civil suit filed for identity theft. On the outside, it seemed like any other data breach. But the language was different. His details had not been hacked—they had been sold. Bundled and sold to overseas customers through intermediary shell companies. The deeper I researched, the more certain I was that it wasn't an accident."

Amore scowled. "And that introduced you to Maxwell?"

Lucius nodded. "Eventually. Every thread led back to him. Dominion. NewTech. Changes of other platforms—all under his influence or backed by the same shadow accounts. But the deeper I went, the more resistant they got. Ideas I pitched got shelved. Editors stopped replying. A few of my articles were published under someone else's name."

"You ghostwrote them," Amore muttered.

"To shield myself," Lucius corrected softly. "The only way I could keep digging. I fed my findings to trustworthy intermediaries. Protected myself in layers. But it wasn't enough. Eventually someone inside caught wind of how close I was getting. The story was killed. My bylines disappeared. Not a scandal, nothing dramatic… just removed."

He paused, lifting his tea again, sipping. "It wasn't like your downfall. Yours was in the public eye. Brutal. Mine was more of a quiet death. But both came from the same hand."

Amore felt a chill of recognition, together with unease.

Lucius continued. "But I stayed in the game. Pursued other leads. Lived small. I never, though, let go of that thread. The humiliation… the betrayal…I was never able to seal that wound shut. I wanted to nail that son of a bitch against the wall for what he took from me. But I had nothing concrete. Just fragments."

He looked at Amore now—entirely. "Then I discovered you. Watched you rebuild. Watched you bleed for the truth. Watched you refuse to disappear. That made you… interesting. It also made you dangerous."

Amore's jaw tightened. "So, what now? You finally step into the light because you see a shot?"

Lucius smiled. "Because I see a mirror."

There was a beat of silence between them that lasted too long. Lucius cut the tension, his voice pitched lower but resolute, sounding exhausted.

"Do you have any notion who we are, Amore?" he asked, not waiting for a response. "We're ghosts. In a world that's only ever going to hear noise."

Amore's brow rose by a fraction, but Lucius wasn't looking at him. His eyes were staring somewhere else, where light was reflecting off the edge of his teacup.

"Journalists," Lucius continued, "real ones—are becoming a dying breed. We are remnants of an era that no longer exists. Truth used to be something sacred. Now? It's just a nuisance. A distraction from the more entertaining lie. We live in a time where it doesn't matter how big or important the truth is, it will always be overshadowed. Because lies are convenient. Easier. They are comfortable. They are babies. The truth hurts too much."

Amore remained silent, his jaw tightening.

"As investigative journalists, we're in everyone's crosshairs. Corporations. Governments. The public. And worst of all, our own egos. Are we doing this for justice? For change? Or just for the next headline? Half the time, I do not even know anymore. What's worse—people no longer care whether something is real or not. They just want to feel like they are right. The average person gets more 'truth' from a viral video than they do from a court transcript. Even facts—real, documented facts—can be dismissed with one phrase: fake news. And the worst part? No one knows what is fake anymore. Not even us."

Lucius stopped, then toned down a little.

"What we do, Amore… it used to mean something. But now? We're digging in a graveyard, hoping to find something still breathing."

Amore shifted in his seat. The words didn't feel dramatic—they felt familiar.

Lucius moved forward once more. "You already lost once. They buried your name in headlines, dissected your credibility. And you survived—barely. But there is not always a second chance. If you go this route again, you had better be certain why. This could be the chance that changes everything. Or it could be your last undoing."

The words hit Amore hard—like gravity, unanticipated and pitiless. He sat with his eyes on the table, mind astray, unseeing. *What am I doing?*

Was this actually about the story, or simply obsession in disguise as purpose?

As he wrestled with the thought, Lucius interrupted him again—almost casually.

"**Dominion**," he said, thumping the side of his bag. "That's one of the firms I'd been investigating."

The name hit like a hammer.

Amore snapped back to attention. "You've looked into them?" he asked, the name still echoing in his mind.

Lucius shrugged, almost too nonchalant. "Off and on. I was tracking a trail through NewTech and a handful of AI-backed firms. Dominion showed up in some filings, some ghost shell investments, some out-of-the-way data harvesting contracts. Could be coincidence. Could be something else."

The air between them shifted. Amore's tone grew cold. "What do you know about the girl? The one who overdosed."

Lucius shrugged, as if fatigued by the tragedy of it. "A sad story. Another girl lost to too many drugs and too many people trying to forget who they are. I do know she died at a Dominion event. That I know for sure. More than that? It's all rumors."

Amore narrowed his eyes. "That's all you've got?"

Lucius struck his bag again. "Not all of it. I have notes. Names. Maybe some threads. But nothing solid. Not yet."

"But you approached me."

Lucius nodded. "Because you've been through the fire before. And because you give a damn—a little more than you want to admit. I have seen your work. I have watched you not walk away. Even when they told you to."

Amore said nothing again.

Then Lucius stuck his hand in his bag and slid a thick envelope down the table. "I've brought everything I've compiled. Notes, references, names. Some of it overlaps with what you have found. But some of it… goes deeper. All I ask is you tread lightly. This isn't journalism. It's survival. You follow this to its end, and it won't be your reputation at stake next time."

Amore didn't move to take it yet.

Lucius let the silence hang a little longer, his voice lowered but steady, sounding exhausted. "This is not a road that you should walk. But one I think you will."

A quiet folded itself over the booth, one that didn't need to be filled. Amore leaned back slowly, looking not at Lucius but at the distorted shadow of himself. His mind wasn't only loud—it was critical. The man sitting across from him could be lying. But what if he wasn't?

He wanted to walk away. To throw his hands up and say: This isn't my fight. I've already been burned. And yet—he couldn't. The very act of staying there, of listening, felt like betrayal. Of what, exactly, he couldn't define. His career? His past self? Or just the fragile peace he had struggled to mend over months? Truth was no longer a virtue. It felt like trespassing into something he shouldn't see. Like breaking and entering—into lives, into secrets, into himself. He stood at a crossroads, and every direction appeared to be a mistake.

Lucius sensed it. Not in Amore's posture—but in the stillness of his soul. And so, without looking triumphant or even particularly hopeful, Lucius limped on. He bent down and pulled the old leather briefcase up beside him and leaned it against his leg.

But first, he said—quietly. "Maybe this was wrong," Lucius said, his voice almost apologetic. "Maybe I shouldn't have come to you. I just thought… you could be a last hope. But I didn't take into account everything. Everything I'd be getting you back into."

He exhaled through his nose, shook his head. "Love and loyalty—they blur things. Make you forget what someone has already had to suffer through. I didn't mean to weigh you down." He began to rise slowly, his hand outstretched for the briefcase, ready to leave Amore with nothing but stifling silence.

But then—

"Stop."

Lucius stood frozen.

Amore's tone was stern, but not frigid. Just determined.

"I want to see it," he said, waving toward the case. "Not that I'll jump back into the fire. Not yet. And not with **Maxwell**—not head-on. Everyone was right. I was too close. Too compromised." He paused, letting the truth hit. "But Dominion… that is different. If your notes contain something— anything whatsoever —I'll sort through them. Just to find out. I owe myself at least that much."

Lucius said not a word. He simply studied Amore as if trying to see past the words, into the fracture lines beneath them. Amore did not blink.

"I'm not doing it for revenge," he continued. "And I'm not doing it to save the world. I'm doing it because something doesn't add up. Lisa—this girl—I don't even know her. But I feel this story. It won't let go."

Lucius let the briefcase fall gently onto the table. "You can read everything," he said to him. "Take your time. No pressure. This doesn't have to be a crusade. Not yet."

Amore felt for it slowly, almost ceremonially. It weighed more than he thought it would. Like the bag wasn't just filled with files.

Lucius made his voice lower, more measured. "And if you require more on Dominion, I can get it. They're going to host another party—some corporate-street fusion nonsense in a few weeks. Because clearly Lisa's death wasn't tragic enough to cancel their social calendar."

He sneered, but it didn't feel performative. It felt personal.

Amore nodded. The lead was real. And now, so was his choice.

"If it leads back to Maxwell," he said quietly, "then… I will cross that bridge when it comes." He rose from the booth, the briefcase in hand.

Lucius stayed seated, but his eyes followed Amore with a strange intensity. Not fondness. Not triumph. Something else.

"We will certainly be in touch," Lucius told him as Amore turned. And then he added, just loudly enough to hang in the air:

"Sooner rather than later."

There was something in his tone—something not a threat. Not a promise. Simply inevitability.

Amore disappeared from the café, the city engulfing him as he vanished. But the weight of that briefcase, and the man within it, trailed behind him like a shadow that would not stretch into the light.

Chapter 14

The Weight We Carry

The briefcase was squeezed tightly against Amore's passenger seat as he gripped the wheel through rush-hour traffic, dodging honking horns and impatient commuters. The city, always in motion, inched along. It didn't care whether he made it to the other side. He made it through anyway, gripping the steering wheel like every second mattered. He didn't just carry information. He carried consequences.

By the time he had walked into his apartment, the sky had darkened and the city below was buzzing. He dropped his keys into the bowl by the door, locked all the bolts out of habit, and placed the briefcase on the table as if it were some ancient relic—like it would speak to him if he leaned in far enough.

It felt heavier than before. A Pandora's box in leather skin. Once opened, it could never be closed. No forgetting what he found, no unknowing the secrets that had waited inside.

Nevertheless, he sat and opened it. The lock clicked open with a sound that echoed louder than it should have.

Papers. Photographs. Clippings. Transcripts. Data logs. Surveillance photos. Names and places scribbled in tight hand-writing, some notes so frantic the pen nearly slashed through the page.

Lucius had been working. Not for weeks—for years.

Amore pulled document after document out onto the table, a mosaic of paranoia, patterns, and power plays. Dominion's name kept surfacing. So did Maxwell. He leaned forward, hand at his chin.

This was real. And somehow, shatteringly familiar. Around the middle of the second folder, he stopped. A document. In his own notes. His own handwriting—sloppy, impulsive, from the beginning of what he knew. It was his paper on Maxwell from his first attempt at the truth. Dated, but piercing.

Amore froze, not stunned by the content, but by the intimate invasion of it. This was an unpublished draft, locked in his old files. *How on earth had Lucius gotten it?* It made clear that Lucius wasn't just watching him; he had breached his life. The revelation settled within him like a numb pain: "If he was observing me this long, why didn't he reach out sooner?" Was Lucius a partner, or a stalker?

He had browsed the pages, feeling a strange ache of nostalgia. He remembered the days he had scribbled down some of those names. "Why didn't you reach out back then, Lucius?" he grumbled to himself, smoothing the corners of a photo stuck to the bottom of an old case file. "We could've taken him down. Together." But maybe that wasn't the problem. Maybe it was guilt. Ego. Or just the isolation of two men cursed with the same affliction—truth.

He sighed, pushing the Dominion folder away from him. This wasn't about Maxwell. Not anymore. This was bigger. Dirtier. He needed to look forward, not backward.

Cross-referenced financial data and anonymous chat logs, and another name was found, Stephen Marks.

The name rang so loudly it hurt. Stephen had been his go-to data analyst during the original Maxwell investigation—a genius with numbers, algorithms, and digital footprints, but slippery. Untrustworthy. He had disappeared when the story had erupted. Amore frowned. Stephen was the only person who could decipher the true meaning of the subtle dips in the data logs—the payment streams that looped instead of ending. Marks knew what they were.

Amore rubbed his temple, reclining in his chair. Finding Stephen again would not be easy. But he had done it before. He would find him again.

He closed his eyes, leaning back on the couch. The room was dark, lit only by the blue light of his phone screen, where Melanie's picture sat in his favorites. He hadn't deleted it. Couldn't. He knew she would answer. Knew her voice could mend the fractured peace he had fought for. *Call her, dummy.* The plea shook him. *You know you need her.* But he clenched the phone in his fist—and slapped it down on the table with a thud of shame. He did not deserve her. Not after what his war had cost her.

He returned to the clutter that covered his desk. Dominion's name scribbled on nearly every page. Buried within were subtleties. Data irregularities.

He closed the briefcase slowly, more deliberately this time. It was no longer a container. It was a decision.

Each page inside it led to something bigger. One receipt had a quote on the payment that read "**restitution prep – MW**." Another sheet of paper talked of "**Phase 3 – network erasure schedule**."

He focused on the Phase 3 document. Something about it would not let go. It established internal names and targets. One of them was given as a contact at Lisa's old company.

His pulse quivered. Coincidence? Perhaps. But coincidences were piling up like breadcrumbs.

He pulled out his phone again. "Naima," he said as soon as she answered. "I need you to cross-check a full set of data for me."

"You okay?"

"I'm okay," lying to himself. "But this briefcase—this information—it's… condensed. I will leave it with you. Just review the entire thing. I want new eyes on this, no matter how credible it looks."

"Full vet?"

"Full," he said. "In depth. Deep dive." He glared again at the Phase 3 document. "I'll mark pages I have to review first. One in particular references a schedule tied to Dominion's systems infrastructure—secured by somebody from Lisa's old firm. That one... that one has to be tracked down."

"You bet," she replied. "You'll get the full run-down."

"Thanks, Naima."

He hung up and gripped the briefcase hard for a moment. It was heavier now—not in his hand, but in his gut. He would trace the patterns. He would follow the leads. And wherever they led him—even if it was back to Maxwell—he would be ready this time. He had to be.

Chapter 15

The Analyst's Echo

Meeting with Naima, Amore thought on the full totality of what he was getting into. This information was such a temptation. He could not turn back, no matter how hard he wanted to. Bringing in more eyes would be helpful, but it would also implicate more people. This was both exciting and dangerous. He had to know how this information came to be. Without hesitation, he knew he needed to go to the source—whatever truth waited there, he was ready to face it.

The phone rang only a few times before it went through. There was the gentle static of the receiver, and then Lucius's voice came through the line, calm and deliberate. "It's good you went over it."

Amore didn't indulge in pleasantries. "That wasn't just a small amount of information. That was years' worth of digging, years of surveillance from internal memos to cross-agency networks. That doesn't just materialize out of a briefcase overnight."

Lucius snickered, low and quiet, as if he were enjoying being confronted. "It took a while. And yes, it was a couple of years in fact. And several channels."

"Yeah, well, I spent years just trying to get a crumb of information out of countless different sources. You compiled at least eight departments' worth of surveillance without even breaking a sweat?" Amore's tone tensed. "You're saying you did this by yourself?"

"I never said I worked alone," Lucius answered smoothly. "I've been keeping an eye on you for years—ever since you became entangled with

Maxwell. My failure caused me to re-evaluate my approach, and it gave me focus."

Amore gritted his jaw. "So what? You are using me to chase your story without any thought for myself. Hell—you are not even considering the legal verifications. This information was collected without proper approval; it's illegal. Do you understand how that will impact me while you play these games? There are consequences to this."

Lucius's tone sharpened. "You didn't chase anything that you didn't already want to chase, Amore. You could always give back my briefcase," he continued. "Walk away. Return everything, forget any of this happened. No one would fault you."

A long pause filled the air.

"So the question is…" Lucius's tone dipped, almost taunting, "Do you really want to?"

Amore's silence spoke for itself.

Lucius didn't hesitate to answer. "I'll speak for you. You may not want to say it out loud—but you want the information. You are going to use it anyway."

The feeling of being right for the wrong reasons burned within Amore. "Why?" he demanded, his voice breaking. "What's in it for you? You could have done all of this yourself. Instead, you dump it in my lap and then just disappear."

Lucius paused. "My gain is irrelevant to this. In the event you are successful, you have more to gain than I do. I am not interested in being a part of a headline. I am more interested in the collapse of the idea."

Amore's irritation did not fade, but beneath it, a deeper unease indicated itself. Lucius wasn't simply a man with know-ledge; he was a man with intention. And his intention had its own destination, whether Amore liked the path or not.

"I have people working with me within Dominion," Lucius continued, his voice soft but precise. "Different sources, from data analysts to independent contractors. Not everyone inside is loyal to Dominion. It's taken me years to build that trust."

"You're building your own network," Amore said, taken aback in amazement.

Lucius didn't deny it. "I'm playing the long game, Amore. You are one of the few people who can move freely enough to make an impact right now. That's why I reached out to you. To be honest, I knew you would look into the information."

"If you hadn't?"

"Then I would have found someone else. But you were the first choice."

Amore stared at the wall of his office, immersed in deep thought. He did not know whether he was being recruited, manipulated, or warned.

Evaluating his options, he had no other choice but to proceed. He had already stared at the point of no return and stepped past it with quiet conviction. Now, it was too late.

"Next time, if there is one," he said angrily, "don't wait until I'm buried knee-deep in this thing before coming clean."

Lucius's laugh was half-hearted. "I have not lied to you, Amore. I have just been mindful with the truth."

With an arrogant, inviting tone, Lucius said, "If you ever need me in the future, I will be here for you. I feel that you will need me at some point."

And then the line disconnected.

The resolve from the conversation with Lucius created more questions than answers. There was nothing he could do right now but meet with Naima. Pulling up to the office, he spotted the familiar glow of her desk lamp through the front window. Approaching the lobby, she was there, as expected, at her desk, fingers furiously striking the keys of her laptop. Her eyes switched between the screen and her notes, sharp and focused, the kind of intensity he knew well.

He dropped the briefcase in front of her as if it might explode.

"Do I want to know what's in that?" she asked, her brow wrinkling.

"Everything," he said. "Or nothing. We have to sort it out."

He snapped the latches open. The moment the briefcase was opened, her smile faded. Her eyes went wide.

"What the hell is all this? This is too clean. Too much. Where did it come from?"

"Where do you think?"

"Lucius." Just saying the name darkened her mood. "You trust him?"

"It's not a question of trust—it's a question of convenience," Amore said. "We're not publishing anything. We are just verifying the information. If it's real, we move on it. If it's not, we bury it."

Naima scanned over the materials with piercing, calculating eyes. Her voice lost its usual steadiness. She sighed. "I have seen shady. I have seen dangerous. But this? This scares me."

"Me too," he said softly, hesitantly. "That's why we're not publishing. But sitting on our hands? That scares me more."

She came to a page entitled **"Phase 3 – Network Erasure Schedule**." "There's a reference here that refers to Lisa's old company."

"I see. We need to double-check everything."

Naima closed the case slowly. "This is a massive amount of information to comb through. You will have what I can find in a few days, but no promises. I have no clue where to start."

As he turned to leave, she shouted back at him, "And what are you going to do if it all checks out?"

He stopped and half-turned to her. "I'll let you know when it does."

Chapter 16

The Search for Stephen Marks

Deep down, Amore realized this task exceeded Naima's abilities. She was an excellent analyst, capable of finding solutions with the best of them, but not on this level of data analysis. It could take her weeks to uncover anything remotely useful. He could not afford to wait that long; time was running out. He needed someone with specific expertise, and a name was already echoing in his mind: Stephen Marks. Marks's inclusion in Lucius's report further piqued Amore's interest. Amore didn't know the importance of this reference—whether Marks could help decipher the data or if it was something else entirely. Marks was a slippery individual, part snake charmer and part data savant. His knowledge and experience were unrivaled in the world of data. He could examine rare statistics, algorithm patterns, and code, and identify issues instantly.

Despite his talent, only two faults defined him: ego and pride. Stephen didn't just want to be right; he had to be seen as legendary. Regardless of the assignment, Stephen would do whatever it took to give a unique spin to the problem. His input was usually insightful, picking up on details others missed. However, the true matter concerning Stephen was basic: what was his benefit? If he believed someone else would succeed and claim credit for his work, he doubled his efforts, not out of concern, but to draw attention to himself. Conversely, if another person proposed a larger incentive, one that stroked his ego, he wouldn't hesitate to abandon you without notice. Pride would always override loyalty for him, and he would even sabotage your achievement just to elevate his own reputation.

This made him both driven and volatile, and thus so dangerous. Yet, he was brilliant, and a resource too valuable to discard. Amore knew he couldn't rely on him—but at the moment, he had no alternative. While working at the *Inquisitor*, Stephen was their point of reference for anything related to data reference. His expertise was instrumental in Amore's first story about Maxwell, yielding results, but when the fallout happened, he vanished. He was needed again now, and the search for Mr. Marks began.

Finding Stephen wouldn't be as easy as it seemed. He had been missing for over a year, and given his methods, he would stay relatively close yet could just as easily disappear anywhere he chose. Looking into his previous home address offered the first sign of progress: he hadn't moved. Records showed he still maintained residence within the city during the past year. That ruled out him settling in another state, but it didn't eliminate the possibility of him going abroad. Scouring documents, public files, and digital trails made it difficult to pinpoint his true location. Knowing this, Amore realized he would have to resort to external means, reaching out to people with superior connections than his own. Finding Stephen would demand more than persistence; it would require strategy.

That afternoon, Amore went to see his old contact, **Dan Rogers**. Entering his office, little had changed about the unassuming slab of frosted glass bearing the worn-out black letters of ***Rogers Investigations***. Dan sat behind a cluttered desk, reading a mystery novel.

"Well, I'll be damned. Look who decides to walk in," Dan said with a grin. "Thought you got too noble for scumbags like me."

"I never pretended to be noble. Just selective," replied Amore. "I need your help; I'm looking for Stephen Marks."

Dan's grin dropped. "Now that is rich; I've been tracking him for another client. It looks like you are not the only person who is looking for him. Someone clearly wants him."

Amore looked up, perplexed. "You don't say. Why is that?"

Dan's expression wavered for an instant. "It's on a need-to-know basis, but I will say the client didn't state a reason why they were looking for him. It's clear somebody wants him desperately."

"You got anything we can work with?"

Dan's grin faltered. "Marks is slippery. Has routines, though. Repeats certain habits when he's anxious. I have been looking into past whereabouts, and I have narrowed it down to a few locations. I will give you a few known hangouts, but what is in it for me?"

Dan turned back to Amore and moved to his desk. "I have known you for years, and you have looked out for me a few times when I needed it, so I will look out for you on this—but it will cost you. The client is looking for him, but there isn't much pressure from their office to get back to me in a timely fashion. I can give you what you want, but I still have to work for the client, since they came to me first."

He wrote three addresses on a piece of paper. Tearing the paper off, he glared at Amore straight in the eye and said firmly, "I'm not doing this for free, Amore. Not now. You want this man; I am providing you with an advantage in my own investigation." I will need something in return—either a large flat fee or a favor in the future. You decide.

Amore took the note without hesitation. "If I get what I want out of him, you'll get what you're owed. Fair?"

Dan's smile was strained and unreadable. "Just don't forget who's giving this to you."

As Amore walked away, Dan added, "If you can get your hands on him, be careful. He is not the same guy you knew. Something has rattled him."

Chapter 17

Closing In

Amore started with the notes Dan had given him: a list of locations scattered around the downtown tech district. They were not high-end facilities, just functional places—coffee shops near coding hubs, libraries with open-access computers, and apartment spaces with short-term leases. Every move Stephen made was careful.

By chance, on the fifth day, gazing out the window of a café, Amore spotted Stephen. He was leaner than Amore remembered, hunched over in a hoodie and constantly checking his surroundings like someone used to being watched.

Monitoring his patterns, Amore was aware that he could approach him, but his present distance from Stephen made confrontation too risky. The only solution was to wait patiently. Although he had to wait a little bit longer, the good news was that he now knew where Stephen was.

It wasn't until the next day that Amore decided to make his move. He finally closed in on him in a shared co-working basement known as **Hexline**. He walked casually through the maze of desks, keeping an eye on each station. Then he saw him. Stephen was at the far end of the room, slumped over two screens, typing away. Amore didn't approach from behind. Instead, he stepped into his peripheral view and waited.

When their eyes met, Stephen tensed. His body froze—not in shock but in acceptance of being cornered. "Amore."

His voice barely carried. "You shouldn't have come here."

"I could say the same,"

Stephen's bravado, which had once worked as his armor now stood shattered. He was the shell of his previous self. In a stunned tone, he bellowed, "I don't have anything!"

Sensing the tension in the air, Amore quickly softened his stance.

"I don't want anything but for you to look over some data," Amore said. "You do that, and I walk away. It will be like I was never here. No one has to know where you are."

After a long pause, Stephen grabbed his backpack, unsure whether to flee or listen, and gave a resigned nod. "What other options do I have?" he grumbled reluctantly. "If I don't go with you, you will notify someone where I am anyway."

"I will go with you, but only if we go back to my place. I would rather not, but this is safer for me there," Stephen said. Questioning if he should, Amore surveyed his choices. This could be a setup. Knowing this was his only chance and not having many options, Amore agreed. Both men walked through the glass doors, neither one truly knowing what to expect next.

Chapter 18

The Proposition

Stephen's apartment was one of the low-end buildings in the area. It was quiet and relatively low-key, the kind of place people might pass without realizing it was an apartment complex at all. Quickly grabbing the briefcase from his car, Amore held it close to his body—just in case something went wrong, and he needed to move fast. His eyes scanned every person nearby, mapping out each exit. He was on full guard. This interaction was high risk.

Stephen wasn't any calmer. If anything, he seemed more jittery than before. Watching his body language, his restless movements, it was hard to tell who was wound tighter between the two of them.

Approaching Stephen's second-floor walk-up, a computer tower sat perched in the corner. Stephen locked the door behind him.

"Why are you acting so paranoid now?" Amore asked.

"I have been involved in different things in the last few months," Stephen replied as he broke off abruptly in the middle of a sentence.

Amore placed the briefcase on the coffee table. As he pulled back his arm, he grimaced slightly from the pain in his shoulder. His expression was brief, but it could not fully hide the discomfort he was in.

Stephen looked directly at him. "Oh, they got to you too, huh?"

Amore was puzzled by the comment. "What do you mean?"

Stephen hesitated, his voice shifting as if he had revealed more than he wanted. "Oh, nothing," he said quickly, almost like a child caught in a lie. "I just noticed you were in slight pain."

Amore responded without hesitation. "Oh, this is nothing—just ran into someone, that's all."

"Alright, that's fine," Stephen said, brushing it off. "Let's take a look at what you've brought me." He flipped open the straps on the briefcase. Stephen opened it with cautious fingers. His fear dissolved into amazement.

"Where in the world did you get this?" he breathed, voice low.

"You're asking the wrong question."

Stephen towered over the papers like a man inspecting live wiring. As he skimmed through the first few pages, his lip tightened, and his breathing quickened. His foot began to tap uncontrollably.

"This… this is Dominion schema. Their encryption tied with their private network. It's not something you just happen to come across."

"I didn't," Amore said. "It was given to me. Can you verify it?"

Stephen laughed once, hollow. "You just don't throw a bomb in my lap and tell me not to ask where it came from. I get everything that's worth keeping hidden, but if half of this is legitimate, you've got something explosive."

"Which is why I coming to you."

Stephen stopped pacing and looked up. "You realize, knowing this kind of thing can lead to real issues."

"I know the risks that are involved."

Stephen nodded, but it was with resignation. "You've been hiding," Amore said, cutting to the chase. "Why?"

Stephen drew a shaky breath. "Let's just say this: whatever I investigated? It does not want to be discovered. And some of what's in this bag… I have seen before. People who dug too deep either disappeared or backed off. Quickly."

Amore didn't flinch. "So?"

Playing to Stephen's ego, Amore leaned back casually and asked, "So, those who looked into whatever you're mentioning—they weren't as skilled as you, is that correct?"

Stephen bristled, his pride flickering across his face. "I do not know their level of skill," he said stiffly, "but I do know they were highly invested in the data."

Amore pressed in, his tone steady but calculated. "They may have been skilled, but they weren't like you. Look, I will respect your privacy about what you were digging into. All I am asking is for you to do me a favor and look this over. I came to you because you are one of the best in the field. Even if you can't find every answer—"

Stephen cut him off sharply. "What do you mean 'can't'? The thing is, I choose not to."

Amore didn't flinch. He let the words hang, then countered evenly. "That's fine. If you choose not to, I just want to know something. Not all of it—just enough to give me an understanding of what I have. Since you know it better than anyone, can you do that for me?"

"So, give me some time. I will dig into it. But if I do this, and I find out that it's real, you'd better be ready for what that means."

Amore sat back, silent. Stephen's pride was forgotten. His charm was restrained, and what was left was a man who knew too much and feared what came next.

Chapter 19

A Cold Warning

Amore could not sleep all throughout the night. The restlessness of his thoughts caused him to constantly sit on the edge of his bed, clutching his phone, waiting for an unexpected call or message. The morning sun had barely crept in, but he had been awake for hours, tossing and turning, trying to predict how the pieces would fall once Stephen and Naima's information was fully processed. The anticipation of the truth was worse than the lie. This was not another story; what he found out stimulated him with countless emotions, which, with the weight of what he felt, threatened to pull him under.

Everything hinged on what came next. If the information was solid, it would reshape his understanding of Lisa's death—and of Dominion itself. But that raised more questions than answers. This was a case of surviving the storm he was about to unleash.

His head spun until his phone buzzed—an unknown number. He picked up. Silence. No sound, no voice, just the dead weight of breathless static.

"Hello?" Amore said sharply.

Click. The call ended.

He creased his brows and glared at the screen. Before he could place the phone back down, it rang again—the same number.

He hesitated, then answered. "Who is this?"

The line was taken up by a low but steady voice with a gravelly accent. It was calm as it whispered, "Amore. It seems you've been very busy lately."

He sat up, his hands tightening on the phone, heart racing against his ribs. "Who the hell is this? How would you get my number?"

The voice brushed off his inquiry. "That doesn't matter. What matters is what comes next. People talk. We hear different versions of things we wanted to believe in. You are looking for something that doesn't want to be found. Let it go. Stop looking into stories that already have an explanation. You have been warned. Besides, don't you have a shoulder that you are nursing now?"

Gripping his shoulder in disbelief, Amore's body tightened up. Enraged, he yelled into the speaker, "I've had threats before. You are not the first, and you damned well won't be the last. But thanks… for telling me that I'm getting close."

He hung up the receiver with a bang, heavily breathing. Threats were one thing, but being able to do physical harm to him was another. The thought of the man in the park resonated with his soul, and the fear that they could have done anything at any time, even worse. But they didn't do anything except give him a warning that day.

Paranoia set in. Everything in his apartment started to feel small. Every noise, vibration, or movement felt like someone coming in to kill him. He had to regroup quickly. Running through his place, he grabbed the few essentials he needed. Without hesitation, he threw on everything for the day and left.

He couldn't decide his next move. Every account he had had begun to creep up in his mind, dating back to the hotel and the feeling of being followed—he could have been followed that day. How did they know? Were they still watching? He needed to find a safe place fast.

Even though adrenaline and panic had set in, he held firmly to his decision: If they want to scare me, they chose the wrong person. This will only be a nail in their own coffin.

As he stepped outside, the feeling magnified. Approaching his car, he spotted two slashed tires. A cold chill ran down his spine. "Oh no. What have I done? If they can come after me, they will come after everyone else. I need to make sure everyone is safe."

Realizing what he had done, dread set in—slow, suffocating, like a hand tightening around his throat. Every choice he had made, every step deeper into this investigation, felt irreversible. There was no clean way out. He had not just crossed a line—he had burned the ground behind him. And now, the weight of what that meant pressed down on him, heavier than the fear itself.

Chapter 20

The Dominoes Fall

"**F**uck, get it together!" he blurted to himself, louder this time, his voice shaking. Amore knew it would not help his situation if he went off emotion, but fear was clawing at him, paranoia buzzing in his head like static. He didn't know what would come next, and the not knowing was worse than anything else. His breath quickened, chest tightening. "It's pointless to stay like this."

Forcing his hands to steady, he snatched up his phone, fingers fumbling across the screen until Naima's contact lit up. He pressed it fast, almost desperate. He couldn't let her be caught off guard. He couldn't risk it. He didn't want to startle her, but the thought kept screaming—he had to make sure she was safe, that she was in a safe place.

He called Naima immediately.

"Hey," he said, attempting to be calm while he panicked. "Is everything good on your end?"

"Yeah, why? You sound weird. What's going on?"

"Just some transportation issues. Slashed tires," he said, trying to keep his composure.

Her tone sharpened instantly. "Are you okay?"

"Yeah, fine. Just… a little bit on edge."

Showing concern, he asked sporadically where she was. Without a doubt, she immediately said, "I am at the office." Amore, being more direct, said, "You need to leave immediately. I don't want anything to happen to you." Sensing the danger and knowing there was more that Amore was not telling her, Naima knew it was in her best interest to leave, and to leave now.

Amore reiterated his demand with a fiery tone. "There is no time for that. I am not ruling out anything. You need to get out now!" Naima answered, "This office is Fort Knox, for the time being. I am changing the security codes as we speak. I've got a monitor on the hallway camera, motion sensors tied into my phone, and a little panic button beneath the desk that'll light up the whole floor if someone so much as makes a move."

"I'll call you in an hour," he said, hanging up.

He tried calling Stephen next. When the analyst picked up, he did not receive a hello. Instead: "Amore. You won't believe what I have been staring at. This data—it's crazy. I will get it all wrapped up tomorrow. But I've seen enough already to know you were right to pursue this."

Amore couldn't help but notice the exhaustion and adrenaline in Stephen's voice—the obsessive energy of a man who had uncovered something too big to walk away from. It was familiar; Amore had heard it in his own voice now. Not wanting to warn him of the danger he was currently in but still curious as to what Stephen had, he said, "Just be careful. If this is what you say it is, they'll be looking for you too."

Stephen gave a hollow laugh. There were still fragments of his paranoia in his voice. "I am moving between places. No one will know where I am. I will text you my location but come at night—and be aware that this is not the same place we went to before."

"Anyway, keep a low profile. Call me when you can."

"Tonight. You'll want to hear this before anyone else."

He hung up.

And yet… fear and anxiety still simmered within Amore. It was not Naima. It was not Stephen. It was Melanie. If anybody was after him, then she was a vulnerability to be used against him. If anything happened to her, he could no longer live with himself. He texted and called, but there was no answer. Images of her lifeless body filled his head.

Feeling that he may be watched and having no transport to himself, the urge to get to Melanie was overwhelming. In an instant, he took off in a flat-out dash. His feet pounded against the sidewalk, moving through different alleys, changing his routines with every turn. The only thought of transportation that entered his mind was his spare motorcycle that he stored away down a couple of blocks within a secure garage. Gasping hard and as if his heart was going to explode out of his chest, at last the garage came into sight.

Huffing for air and shaking, he punched in his code, the click of the keypad sounding louder than a gunshot in the silence. The lock clicked shut. He yanked open the door, bolted inside, and fell across the motorcycle. The quicker he turned the key and got it moving without hesitation.

Chapter 21

An Unspoken Farewell

When he reached her apartment, he ran up the flight of stairs until he made it to her door. Outside, he knocked twice. Nothing. He knocked harder. Yelling just enough that she could only hear, he shouted, "Melanie?" Still nothing. His voice cracked, louder this time. "Mel?" Then finally, at last, the sound of the lock turning.

She opened the door, startled. "Amore? What the hell? Why are you knocking like that?"

"I called you, and there was no answer," he said, letting out a sharp sigh of relief he had not realized he was holding until he saw her face.

"Sorry, I had my headphones on and did not hear the phone. What's wrong?" she asked. Noticing he was out of breath and had run a flight of steps to get to her, Melanie knew something was wrong, her eyes cutting through his lame excuse.

He shook his head, looking over her shoulder into her apartment. His chest throbbed, but he forced the words out: "I was in the area. I don't know. Maybe. I just needed to check that you were okay. I had a feeling something was wrong, that you were in danger," he said uncertainly.

Her eyes narrowed, suspicion sharpening her tone. "That's a façade. Don't lie to me. You weren't in my area. And why would I be in danger? You are out of breath, and you just randomly show up at my place."

With resignation, she said, "You are on another crusade, aren't you?"

Unable to hold up his appearance and feeling her in his presence, Amore with a heavy heart said, "Yes, I am on another story, but can we talk about this more inside?"

Entering her place, a wave of nostalgia hit Amore, as though he was in a place where he felt like he was where he needed to be, but he knew it wasn't right.

Melanie asked, in an open-ended tone, "Why haven't you called me? Why haven't you reached out to me in these past few months, and now you are here?"

He began to speak. "It was for your protection."

She crossed her arms. "You didn't call once you had left me. You didn't say anything to me, and the one thing that I can say I am guilty of is trying to be there for you when you needed me. And now you show up talking about threats. Don't use that line. You didn't leave to protect me. You left because you were scared, I'd stay."

That lingered. He looked away, guilt creeping under his skin. "You're not wrong. I am sorry."

"You were always looking for something bigger than the two of us. A story," she said in frustration. "I only wanted the parts of you that didn't need to be published."

Silence stretched, thick but familiar. She poured him a glass of water.

"You still care," he asked.

"I'll always care," she said, her voice steady. "I just don't know if you still do."

He looked directly at her, speaking with quiet weight. He said, "I think about you every day. There is so much I could say in this moment, things that I have been thinking about just by being in front of you, but I can't find the words to say how I truly feel—only that I love you, and this is the hardest thing I have had to do. And I am sorry. For everything."

She reached out, touching his hand softly. "You still don't get it. I wasn't afraid of your problems. I was afraid you didn't want me in it."

His eyes stung, but he nodded. "After this—after this case—I'm done. I just want peace again and I want you back in my life."

"You've never been good at peace," she said, smiling sadly.

He took a step closer, hugging her tightly. Inhaling the scent of her perfume, the warmth of her body. It reminded him of the man he used to be. Of the man he could be again.

She whispered in his ear. "Don't be a stranger, Amore. You never know… I might be gone too."

He let her go, took a step back, and turned away.

Outside, the sun was setting—but the storm was just beginning.

As the door closes behind him, the click of the lock sounding so much louder than it should have, Amore exhales slowly, the warmth of Melanie's embrace still on his chest, reminding him of what could have been. Relief courses through his veins—she's alive, untouched, safe—but tempered with a harsh strain of truth. The moment offered clarity, not comfort.

He loves her. That's the truth, and the truth is a dangerous thing.

His footsteps felt heavier as he walked into the night, weighed down by the sobering reality that the love which burns between them is precisely why he can't be with her. Not now. Maybe not ever.

Her safety wasn't just a question of his personal comfort; it was a bitter reminder. The moment she opened the door, her eyes looking worried and her voice laced with concern, Amore knew: if someone had harmed her because of him, he would never forgive himself. Not even in death.

Love was no longer love. Love was leverage. And in this game, leverage is what gets you killed.

So, he locks it all away; the pain of the fragile dream. If this were ever his last case, he needed to finish it clean. He needed to finish it alone.

Sitting on his bike in a secluded spot off to the side of the parking lot, leaning forward over the handlebars and trying to calm his nerves, deep inside he thought he needed to stop—everything was becoming too much to bear. His body ached, his mind was cluttered. It was crazy for any human being to think that it was wise to continue. But he couldn't stop. He needed to get through it.

Having Melanie safe, his thoughts switched over. Naima. He needed to make sure she was fine.

He pulled out his phone, hands trembling a bit as he dialed her number. He pinned the phone to his ear, waited, the seconds ticking by. Finally, she answered.

"Hey, are you okay? Where are you?" he asked, words spilling out the instant the line connected.

"I'm fine," she replied, a bit winded but steady. "Back at my place, looking over the information. This story is becoming dangerous."

Her tone made his chest tighten. With great emphasis, he said, "I think it's probably best that you are not involved with this anymore."

There was a pause, and then she spoke more harshly. "This is not new to you. And I've seen you when you've been locked into something. You keep on, no matter the price. But…" she let out a breath, softer now. "I see."

"I never said I'd stop," he muttered, the voice low, the exhaustion weighing on each word. "I just want to make sure this is for your safety."

On the other side, there was a silence—he could almost hear her thinking. And then, with a trace of disappointment in her tone, she said, "I believe you're right. But I've seen some things while going over the data. I left the key to the main evidence safe behind. It's too critical to abandon. I had to rush out of there and didn't have time to pick it up before I left."

Amore stood up on his bike, teeth clenched. "You have to quit," he said roughly. "But if you want to share this information with me, I will pick it up from the office later and meet you at your place sometime soon. For now, you must keep a low profile."

Without a response, the silence speaks volumes. They conclude the call.

Stephen had insisted on choosing the location. The directions were complicated with three changes to where he was in transit. Arriving at a private loft, he proceeded to a service elevator that groaned as if it hadn't been moved in decades, and a narrow corridor that ends in a locked door, only opening after being buzzed in. Inside, the room was all walls and concrete with a bare bulb dangling from the ceiling.

"You made sure no one followed you?" Stephen asks before Amore can speak.

"Wouldn't be here if I didn't," Amore replies with sarcasm.

Stephen's laptop was already open; its screen littered with different windows. His hands move with the practiced speed of someone who thinks faster than most people speak.

"I've been at this all day since you left," Stephen began speaking, his voice low but thrumming with pride. "Everything you've been chasing— it's not just fragmented data. At least, not the one you're searching for. The patterns exist—same corporate overlap, same shadow transfers—but it's too much to unravel without more access. I can report that they're all sourcing it out to the same place. It's an entire distribution structure. Multiple companies, multiple industries, all shuffling information like a shell game. And somehow, all of it… ends up in one place."

"One place?" Amore asks.

Stephen gives a dry laugh. "Yeah. Which is insane. We're talking about data volume that should be impossible to centralize. And the encryption? It's like someone poured concrete over the code and then welded steel over that. I am barely scratching the surface, and that's me talking. You would need ten more people with my level of expertise to even start on cracking a fiber of the code."

Arrogance laces his words, but it can't hide his fear of what he was saying.

Amore leans forward. "You mentioned before you've seen something like this."

Stephen freezes on a keystroke. "I… might have. Years back. Different company. Another name. But the patterns? The way the data moves, it had the same fingerprints. Back then, I thought I was digging into some boutique analytics shop. But it… connected."

"To Dominion?"

Stephen's eyes flick up. "I did not say that."

"You didn't have to."

For an instant, the room felt smaller.

Stephen reclines, massaging the bridge of his nose. "There's more. Your Lisa—she's listed in the files. Not labeled as 'Lisa,' but as a handler. Cross-referenced with several individuals in media and PR. I pulled a list."

He turns the laptop toward Amore. Names roll down the screen, some of them familiar, some buried deep in corporate secrecy. Near the top, Amore catches it; Duvall.

"That explains the party," Amore sighs.

"Maybe," Stephen says. "Or maybe not. The fact is, the list does not tell us what she was doing, only that she was connected. And that's bad enough."

Amore took Stephen's flash drive, feeling its slight weight in his hand. Stephen's fingers hovered above the keyboard, a ghostly movement of one already gone.

"I don't get it," Amore said, the words were flat. "You're walking away from this?"

Pacing as he spoke, he could not keep the excitement out of his voice, or the fear. His movements were jerky, restless, as if a man trapped in his own skin. "Do you know what you've gotten yourself into? This is not something you mess around with. I've stumbled into it before, and I don't want any part of it," he said to Amore with a stone-cold indifference, fear very much carved upon his face.

His voice dropped, almost a threat. "You have to let this go. I've met people that had stumbled into this at some point in their lives, and all of a sudden disappeared. Vanished, like that." He paused, his eyes darting as if expecting someone to burst into the room. "I came close to that myself, closer than I ever want to be again. And I do not want any part of this."

Stephen's expression was unreadable as he looked up. "Our deal," he said, the words sharp. "Remember? I would look at your data. I have. I'm making good on my side of the bargain—no strings attached, nothing more, nothing less."

"You have a chance to take down something massive," Amore countered, his voice rising with disbelief. "Something that's haunted you for years. The glory alone—you have lived for this."

Stephen emitted a short, dry laugh. "You're right. I do. But this isn't about glory. You've got enough information here to give as much away as you can. You've got to be careful, Amore."

Amore's eyes glinted. He understood the words, but he couldn't grasp the true magnitude of what Stephen was saying. Stephen was tenacious, competitive, and egotistical, which he craved to be the best. The fact that he was abandoning a case of this size, one that was personally connected, meant that something was seriously wrong.

Stephen moved closer in, his voice a cautionary tone. "I am keeping my word. I will disappear after you leave. Just do me one thing: you need to move like a man that has everything to lose. And trust me, you do."

Amore nodded hesitantly, keeping to their agreement and the underlying threat behind it. "I'll keep my word, too, and won't let anyone know where you are for the time being."

Chapter 22

Box In

Leaving the loft, the reality was brutal and clear: this was no random death—it was murder. Stephen's revelation had validated his worst fears: Lisa's death was no accident. A new, terrifying reality had taken root, one that was bigger and far more sinister than he could possibly have imagined.

Adding to the tension were the threats, the slash tires and the chilling warnings that there was no safety for those he held dear. There was a desperate need for justice, but a cold reminder told him this was bigger than he was. He couldn't simply barge in on a theory and a hunch. Nevertheless, he knew one person who held the key to all this madness: Dax Duvall. Duvall was the center of the problem, the calm in the eye of the storm, but he had not been heard from in weeks, a ghost on the airwaves.

It seemed like a dead end. There was no easy decision that would bring him peace. Combing deep stretches of his mind, he was lost for any actual solutions. He had the information Stephen gave him, but there was only so much he could accomplish from it. It gave him some direction, but nothing groundbreaking in the eyes of the public. Maybe there was something he had overlooked.

Recalling his earlier conversation with Naima, he laid out a plan: he would return to the office, retrieve the files she had left behind, and then visit her once more tomorrow. Afterward, he would then compare her files with Stephen's information. It was only a starting point, but for now, it was the best course of action he had. Weaving in and out of the streets in the dark night, pressing forward to his office, his movements cautious and deliberate. He couldn't risk being seen.

Arriving in the rear of the building, he used the back door and mounted the stairs, a silent ghost in the night. As he reached the visitors' lobby, he could see his office door opened, greeted by one of utter chaos. Trash was scattered everywhere. This wasn't a random search; it was a targeted hunt for something specific.

Standing there, he was petrified with fear. He could retreat the way he came, but there was no telling if someone was outside waiting for him to come back. Every nerve screamed at him to run, but the memory of him hitting the ground during his jog; the pain in his shoulder kept him frozen, pinned between the threat he knew and the unseen one outside. Cornered and trapped, there was no reason to just stand there. His heart sank. He had no clue if the intruder was still there or not. If they were there, he needed protection, and he had that in the form of his gun hidden within his desk.

On high alert, he stepped forward, a mouse in a kitchen full of cats. His eyes searched the room. He couldn't leave, not knowing he could have done something more. He braced himself and crawled to his desk, his only thought to get his gun in a secret compartment below.

A sudden sharp, loud sound from the back room broke the silence. A thud. He lunged for the desk, survival mode kicking in. His hand wrapped around the cold metal, and a surge of courage coursed through him. Now armed, he would not go quietly into the night. His eyes scanned wildly, his heart a frantic beat against his chest. He didn't know who was there, but he knew this was it.

He cautiously turned the corner, gun held high. He saw a figure darting out from the neighboring office. He didn't know if anyone else was there. Holding the gun close to his chest, his finger over the trigger. "If you're still in here," he shouted into the void, his voice trembling with a deadly resolve, "you'll be carried out in a body bag!"

Driven by a mix of adrenaline and fear, he moved from his office into the darkened corridor. Each corner was a potential threat. The gun in his hand felt both heavy and comforting at the same time. Determined, this was not how his story would end. He swept through the building, on high alert, combing for anyone who was suicidal to come for him.

He was overcome by a wave of relief that didn't last long. An eerie calm fell over the building, a forced silence that was not safe. Nothing was in motion but his own footsteps echoing too loud in the silence. Head on a swivel, Amore moved from room to room with calculated caution, each step measured, each glance sharp. The emptiness felt staged, unnatural, as if someone had cleared the space just moments before. The intruders were gone, but the chaos they had caused was a bitter reminder that they had been there.

Still on edge, Amore looked around the space to ensure he was truly alone. If someone was there, even if they had been left behind, something would have been there—a shadow shifting, a breath caught in the air. Yet nothing was there. The deeper he pushed through the building, the tighter the air seemed to cling to him. Navigating each of the rooms, it became evident—temporarily, at least—he was not here with anyone else. But the silence did not provide relief. It brought a deeper dread, one that shouted: "If they were not here now, then they would be waiting somewhere else."

"What the hell were they looking for?" he demanded, exasperation in his tone. "And how did they know to look here?"

The questions remained, the answer as obvious as if it was horrifying. He had been set up, and the person responsible for everything had to be Lucius. Ever since the day he had walked into Beyond Reach flaunting information about his past or stumbled upon this briefcase, his life had turned into chaos of questions and unseen threats, and now Lucius was nowhere to be seen. A look through the debris confirmed his suspicion; they were looking for the briefcase.

"Where is it?" he asked tensely. Looking back at the text from Naima, she told him that she had managed to get it secured into one of their safes before she left. Talking to himself, the questions still remained: "The only person who could have known Naima would put it in the safe—the only person who could be tracking my every move since day one—was Lucius," he thought. "But why would Lucius set me up just to give me the briefcase?" wanting to know. "And why would he hold on to it in the first place? Maybe I am jumping to conclusions too quickly."

His phone buzzed. He looked down and saw Lucius's name on his phone. Anger rushed through him. He picked up the phone. "You bastard! Why did you do this?" he yelled.

On the other end, Lucius's voice was frantic. "Are you alright? We've been compromised! We need to meet urgently. This is no game!"

Concern replaced his anger. "Are you okay? Where are you?"

"I'm on my way to somewhere safe," Lucius said, his voice now a low, hurried whisper. "I'll text you a location when I'm in a safe spot. We need to regroup and figure out our next move. I'll text you once I'm safe." The line went dead. The noise of frantic movement could be faintly heard in the background.

It was after midnight when Lucius's message flashed across the screen. There was no greeting or explanation, just a stark address: "2712 Copper Inn Road. Be there within the next hour."

Amore's stomach tightened. Copper Inn Road. A busy strip on the outskirts of the city, known by night for its jam-packed clubs. During the day, it's a place full of people enjoying the restaurants and entertainment. Why there, of all places? The location seemed too exposed, too dangerous. If Lucius was really in danger, why pick a spot so out in the open?

Hesitation gripped Amore, phone still in his hand and his mind racing. Caution screamed in every impulse. Lucius was his only link to the truth, the one man who possessed all of information that could unravel everything. He had no other choice. Without him, the investigation would stall to a screeching halt. Getting there would not be a problem, but at this time of night, the place would be deserted, making them both easy targets. Too much open ground, too little cover. He had to be careful.

He slipped on his jacket, felt the gun holstered beneath his car seat. He wasn't going unarmed. He took a deep breath, started the engine and drove slowly, meticulously checking his mirrors. The city was another place at this hour, its energy beneath the surface. Amore kept an eye on the mirrors, every pair of headlights in his rearview mirror making him think he was being watched. Instinct or paranoia? He chose to be safe rather than sorry, pulling into a parking lot for a warehouse. He switched off his headlights, pulled into a secluded corner, and killed the engine. The quiet of the area closed in around his senses.

He sat in the darkness, the silence of the grounds amplifying his unease. No cars, no people. A good sign, but a dangerous one. He was exposed. He waited a bit more, then opened the door slowly, his eyes searching the empty lot. It felt like an eternity before he finally stepped out, his eyes fixed on every shadow and every nook.

Then, a figure emerged from the darkness. It was Lucius.

Lucius remained cautious, his head swiveling and his eyes darting as if he expected to be attacked at any moment. His demeanor was altered—less frantic, more resolute. He moved to Amore and, without stopping, grumbled, "Come closer." Amore moved toward him, feeling a tightness in each step he took.

"What's going on? Why are we here? What danger are you in?" Amore's inquiries came out in a hushed rush.

Lucius didn't answer. He gazed past Amore, scanning the perimeter, and simply nodded toward the closest parking garage. His silent communication spoke volumes.

Anticipation hung thick in the air within the garage. Lucius stopped and turned to Amore, his tone was now firm and authoritative. "Are you sure that you weren't followed?"

"Yes. It's just me. Now, tell me what's going on."

Lucius's manner changed, his body language becoming tense, almost predatory. He pushed Amore against a concrete pillar, his voice low and insistent, with desperation. "Someone tried to break into my apartment while I was there. My cameras alerted me, and I barely escaped. But I have no clue how they discovered me."

The next thought entered Amore's head. "You, too?" Lucius's gaze was unwavering. "While outside of my building, I was about to call you for answers when I noticed two cars speeding up behind me. I had to get away. That's when I knew something was wrong. I phoned you so that we could address this."

"At first, I thought it was you," Lucius admitted, his eyes unflinching. "But when I saw the two cars... no. This is bigger. Somebody tipped them off."

Confused, Amore was speechless. They were both being targeted. If it was not Dominion or Maxwell pulling the strings, then who was it? And how did they know about them? Amore voiced the question that hung in the air: "Then who is it?"

Lucius became agitated. He pushed a hand through his hair, muttering. "I don't know! I spent years gathering that information, and now I have people after me. I figured at first it was you, but now I see I'm wrong."

Taking a deep breath, Lucius began to process the events. His face showed a tremendous burden as he muttered to himself. "Who could it be? Which one of them betrayed me? No, it wasn't him. It couldn't be him... What about Tommy?" His voice frayed at the edges until he steadied himself. "The reason I called you here is because we can't wait. This is the moment where there is no turning back. One of us is likely to be killed if we do not act first.

"What are you suggesting?" Amore asked, his curiosity roused.

Lucius leaned in. "I told you before, I still have people inside Dominion. That's how I gathered all this information. A few of them want to expose what has happened, but they're scared. I arranged a meeting with my top contacts in the organization. Under the disguise that Dominion is hosting another party in the next few days, we will meet in plain sight. It's the only place they will feel safe to talk. While they are having the time of their lives, we will be planning the fall of Dominion. I have an invitation. If you want to go, we can survey the scene and get more intel."

"That's suicide," Amore shot back. "If people were searching for us, why would we willingly walk into the lion's den?"

Amore's voice was a mix of frustration and genuine concern as he faced Lucius in the dim light of the parking garage.

"Because it's the one place we'll be safe to meet my contacts," Lucius answered, his voice cold with certainty. "It's all set. Besides, after Lisa's death, they cannot afford something to go wrong. They will never let anyone who is not invited get in through the front door. Security will be heightened. We hide in plain sight. We're safer in there than we would be on our own. Plus, by connecting with my contacts, I can flesh out all the information we have. We'll get closer to the truth than ever before. One night. One chance. Nobody would be suspicious. Once we get in and get out, we can form a plan to expose everything."

He continued, the name a venomous disdain: "Everyone will be there—Executives, politicians, media moguls, including Maxwell himself."

That name sent a jolt through Amore. "With your briefcase, I had been quietly working on your own leads. I've been digging into the briefcase. I have someone analyzing the data. He found patterns. Connections," Amore said, his interest stirred.

Lucius eyed him, suspicion sharpened, pushing for more. "Who is this insider? What resources do you have, and what exactly have you discovered?"

"I have someone who has the expertise to interpret this information. He took a look at it and gave me some good insights."

Lucius's suspicion returned. "How much does your inside guy know?"

Amore's expression remained guarded, his loyalty to Steven unwavering. "When the time is right, you'll know. Until then, we stay the course. I am interested to see where this goes. Once we have answers and solid facts, then I'll disclose my sources." The unspoken implication was that if this panned out, he'd have to locate Steven again, a problem he'd address when the time arose.

A tense silence stretched, then Lucius gave a single, firm nod. "Fine. We'll play it your way. So, I assume you're going to the party?"

"Yes, set up my invitation," Amore stated, his focus sharpening. If Dax was there as well, which gave him even more motivation, this would be a great opportunity to kill two birds with one stone.

Lucius moved towards the parking garage exit. "I will call you later with your invitation. This is a party full of executives and media personalities, so you need to dress the part. Keep your head down and listen. Clean yourself up and learn to mix with the crowd." Lucius headed for the exit, his voice echoing in the parking deck. "The party is two days from now. Once I have everything that I need, we will meet."

Amore, speechless but focused, gave a silent nod of agreement. The two men left as suddenly as they came, watching each other as they exited the premises.

Amore followed, his mind racing with thoughts. "This is it. Everything I've been working towards. This is where the rubber meets the road," Amore muttered to himself. "When I get there, I will nail everyone involved. And if I have enough information, I'll finally be in a place to catch Maxwell."

Chapter 23

The Underbelly of Deception

Two days leading up to the party dissolved into a blur of frantic preparation. Amore had to embody the wealth he despised, acquiring Italian suits and exquisite cologne to blend in. The cost exceeded his budget, but he saw it as the only course of action. This necessity mirrored the chilling precision of Lucius, his surprising collaborator, who worked tirelessly behind the scenes. Lucius acquired fabricated names and false authorities, moving with an intensity Amore almost admired, ensuring their entry. Amore did not truly know this man, but he saw a mirror of his own dangerous resolve.

With their access secured, Lucius also acquired a copy of the guest list. Amore and Lucius scrolled through the names, which included some of the biggest figures in the industry. Some were figures Amore had only ever heard of, seemingly larger than life, and others so unexpected that he was amazed to discover that they would be in the same vicinity. It was a stark reminder that public appearances often hide what truly happens behind closed doors in the lives of the rich and famous.

The night of the affair was shrouded in secrecy. Cloaked in mystery, being invited meant a place that could not be found. Everything was coordinated to the detail, all the way to the second. The organizers had gone to absurd lengths, based off the heat they received from Lisa's death—not out of remorse, but to protect their reputation.

The first stage of arrival required guests to arrive at a rundown, abandoned building that seemed to be in the middle of nowhere. Badges were scanned for entry, but this was only the first step. Guests were then shuttled in various cars to another dilapidated building, this one in the heart of the city. Upon entering, security and people who looked like drifters pushed guests toward a secret corridor leading to a long hallway.

Amore was filled with disbelief. Emerging from the hallway, he stepped into a luxurious, sprawling space—a covert world. The building was a maze of various rooms, its luxurious inside wildly contrasting its exterior. This was a high-descent trip curated by people who had no boundaries, thriving on bending reality for appearances. It was packed with well-known celebrities, athletes, executives, PR representatives, and CEOs.

Upon entering, a concierge welcomed him and Lucius at the entrance. "Mr. Rutherford, thank you for coming." Almost taken back by the greeting, Amore looked down at his credentials as if he was fixing his shirt while confirming that he was talking to the right person. Glancing briefly, he could see the name Brian Rutherford with his photo glimmering against the plastic. Not wanting to cause suspicion, he played along with the man, who came across as if he had been used to doing this all night—merely looking at the badge when the guests arrived to show hospitality. "If you require anything, just notify us, and we will gladly comply," the servant said. In a stoic manner, Amore thanked the man and continued on. Every interaction felt superficial. A profound disgust stewed within Amore, knowing he was going to have to share a space among such individuals who only performed when the camera was on them.

The venue was meticulously structured with assigned areas, each tailored for various "fun activities." Rooms were specialized for whatever indulgent tastes were craved. One room offered a choice of men and women for taking part in any type of fetish. Other rooms were designated for drugs, showcasing different preferences and broken down by the type of substance for the type of high you wanted to experience. The sight was a sickening spectacle: a renowned mega-church pastor could easily be found indulging in sex with the opposite sex.

Drugs and alcohol flowed freely. People indulged in their deepest desires out in the open, having sex without a care in the world. Lucius had been with him but was lost in the crowd. Amore was on his own, attempting to navigate the craziness. He could not help but feel a journalist's impulse—to expose it all—yet he knew a story revealing this truth behind the powerful would never be published.

With Lucius gone, Amore set his mind on locating Dax. With countless rooms and guests indulging in various activities, this was a formidable test. The air was thick with smoke, and laughter bled into shouts. He pushed through it all, working his way through the chaos, casually socializing with partygoers to pick up on a sense of where Dax was.

The music was a loud, blasting bass beat, vibrating through the walls. People drifted in small groups, their laughter punctuated by the atmosphere. At the center of one group was Flex, as to be expected, the center of attention. Even without a camera on him, Flex was always "on," a relentless showman. From afar, Amore could perceive how exhausting this had to be—an endless, thankless job of wearing a mask and changing your persona for whoever was in front of you. It was a journey that could end in losing yourself in the process, but Flex played the part of the chameleon flawlessly

Amore slowly drifted into the crowd surrounding Flex. With a gradual nudge against Flex's back, he created an opportunity, apologizing profusely. "I didn't see you there. My mistake, I truly apologize. Oh my god, are you Flex the streamer? I'm a huge fan!"

Modesty was not one of Flex's traits. "Yeah, I am him," he replied with a smirk, fully taking the bait. "Man, you wilding—nah, you crazy!" he yelled, slapping a friend on the back before taking another gulp of his drink. Amore waited for a break in the conversation. "You know Dax, don't you?"

Flex spun around quickly, his grin still intact. "Dax? Yeah, that's my guy! Cool dude, sharp with it, too. I've partied with him a few times. Why, are you pressing about him or you trying to link up or something?" He laughed and shook his head dismissively. Amore joked back, "Yeah, I want to link up with him. I have some projects in the works, but he hasn't been seen in the last few weeks. Maybe something that's in the air. But if he's here, I'd love to speak with him."

Flex cocked his head, a playful but suspicious glint in his eye. "I hate to tell you this, but you are coming on too strong, bro. Why don't you just contact his people? They have managers for that. PR people. That's their lane, not mine." Amore nodded his head once, a deliberate one. "I heard he was here, and I haven't had a chance to bump into him. Just wanted to know if you've seen him. That is not the route that I am going for. You, if you are cool with him, you may have a tendency of seeing him before me that will lead him in the right direction. That's why if you see him, then you can introduce me."

Flex blinked, then let out a sharp, nasty laugh. "Hold up, no, you're sounding like you're ordering me around! What's this, am I your side mission? You trying to unlock Dax like he's a hidden character or something? Come on, bro." The grin remained, but his eyes opened in suspicion, scrutinizing Amore's face. Amore's tone stayed low, level, only loud enough for Flex to hear. "This isn't funny. Consider it a favor for me. If you do this, he'll understand. And when this project blows up, you will too. Eventually." Flex let out a half-chuckle, shaking his head as if to brush it off, but the amusement didn't reach his eyes. Amore was already stepping away, disappearing into the crowd before Flex could move.

"Favor," Flex muttered to himself, his smile slanting downward as he looked at his drink. He quickly looked down at Amore's credentials, his mind instantly shifting. "Sorry, I didn't know who you were. Didn't you work for a firm in Dominion once?" Taking advantage of the mistaken identity, Amore played along smoothly. "Yeah, but I've moved around a lot since then. Do you know where Dax is?" Flex explained, "So, that project you want to talk to Dax about—are we talking good money? Cause if so, that might be up my alley. Always trying to get a good percentage." Amore grinned, leaning into the mood. "Yeah, we can work out the details with you in the future. Let me talk with Dax first, and before I leave, we can make something happen." Flex continued, "Yeah, he's somewhere around here. Let me put a word out, and I'll find him and get back with you. Where are you going to be?" "Just around," Amore said. "No need, you can stay with me," Flex told him. "It should only take a few minutes.."

Chapter 24

A Drunken Meeting

Less than a second after Amore's proposition, one of Flex's entourage leaned in close and whispered in his ear. Flex's expression shifted subtly, and he casually approached Amore. "Dax is in one of the back rooms," he said with great enthusiasm. "We can go catch up with him, but first let me get you a drink. Since we're just becoming buddies and to our future partnership, I want to commemorate this moment"

He snapped his fingers, and a servant immediately appeared with two glasses of bubbling champagne. Bubbles danced all the way to the rim. Amore felt a wave of hesitation; he didn't want to drink. He glanced over at Flex and his entourage. Each one had a drink in their hands, and they were fixated on him with vacant stares, as if he was the odd man out

Flex broke the silence. "You don't want to drink? You're not going to commemorate this moment? Are we not cool?" The pressure was on. Amore knew declining the invitation would generate suspicion. He grabbed the glass and clinked it against Flex's. "To new beginnings," he stated, and drank the cold liquid.

" You're cool," Flex said with a wide grin creasing his face. "I need your contact information before you leave. We can link up. I have some ventures down the line. How can a man of your expertise help me with my platform? I'm stretched thin with my team, and with new developments entering the new year, I would want to have your eyes on things."

Amore, not knowing how to respond or how deep this conversation might go, cut it short. "Yeah, we can definitely work something out after the party. Get my information on your way out." This was a chance to add Flex to his list. Clearly intoxicated and not fully aware of who Amore was, this was an opportunity to gain more information in the future since he had connections within the organization. He would have to cross that bridge later.

Down a flight of stairs and into a private room filled with nothing but women and drugs, there he was: Dax, slumped over in the corner. He was relishing the festive atmosphere, but his demeanor suggested he was either coming up from a high or had already reached its peak. His speech was inebriated and sluggish.

Dax's appearance was not what he appeared like on air. His forehead was drenched in sweat, soaking through his shirt. It was impossible to tell if it was his own perspiration or as if someone had dumped a bucket of water on him. His eyes were ghost-like, locked in a trance, lips moving with broken mumbles as he forced a smile onto his face.

Flex caught Amore watching and raised a hand. "Let me talk with him first before I introduce you. He's having a good ride right now, and I want him to fully know you before you come up. Is that cool?"

Amore, seeing the man's fragile state, stepped back, waiting for a proper introduction. The room felt hotter by the second, sweat beginning to slip down his own forehead.

Then Flex broke the tension with a booming shout. "Dax, my guy! You letting these women get you off your game. I know you're enjoying yourself, but I want to introduce you to someone." He reached out, clasping Dax's hand, tugging him upright with a firm pull.

The two tussled playfully, though Dax's movements looked loose, almost too loose, like a man unmoored. Still, his voice rose in a cheerful tone. "Flex, this party is lit. Why are you interrupting me to talk to someone? Let's find some women to get our rocks off."

"We definitely want to do that," Flex laughed, though his tone carried an edge. "But here's the rep I was telling you about. He's going to brighten our futures."

Flex approached Amore with Dax. "This is the guy who has been looking for you, Rutherford. I wanted to introduce you two." Getting himself more composed, Dax uttered in a sluggish tone, his words dragging like he was half there, half lost in the haze. "You're the guy that's going to make me a lot of money with this new deal, right? Flex has been hyping you up, so let's party!"

He raised his voice, shouting into the blur of music and laughter. "Let's have some fun!"

At his call, topless women began to emerge from the crowd, weaving their way toward him with seductive smiles. Their voices overlapped each other: "Yes, daddy, whatever you want, we're down for a good time." The heat in the room seemed to thicken, the bass vibrating off the walls, sweat and music mixing into a dizzying haze.

Amore, seeing exactly where this was headed, stepped in quickly to defuse the situation. His tone was steady but firm, trying to redirect the moment before it unraveled. "Before we get into all that, let's sit down and talk, and I can run down what I propose."

Flex, unfazed and drunk on the chaos, snatched one of the women by the waist, pulling her against him with a wild grin. His laugh tore through the noise, loud and hysterical. "If you guys are all business, that's no fun for me!" "I'm heading back to the party, but make sure you let me know how things go." With a quick wave, he walked away. Just as he left, he shot Amore a look that was both a promise and a coded message. "I'll definitely be getting with you before you leave," he answered in an encrypted fashion that only Amore would understand.

Feeling as if his body was slightly heavier, he ushered them both to a corner where they could sit down and talk privately without any distractions. Noticing the heat of the room, Amore signaled to one of the servers to bring two glasses of water. Dax was awkwardness personified, but Amore, being the pro that he was, didn't react. Rather, he scanned the room, taking a read of the mood. Dax was in a vulnerable state and would let it all hang out. Amore knew he had to take his words with a grain of salt. It was risky being that he was high on drugs, but Amore was fixated: he was the closest he'd ever been to knowing what happened to Lisa.

Dax was in a cheerful, talkative mood after a sip of water, his words more animated than usual. He was a caricature of a television personality, swagger and confidence personified. "I've heard so much about you," Amore said to him, "I'm a huge fan!"

Amore continued: "I've heard some rumors that you were on hiatus, but someone with a talent like yours shouldn't be off the air. Where have you been hiding for the last few weeks?"

"Oh, you know, I took a vacation—a sabbatical, whichever you want to call it. I'll be back in no time, but meantime, it's a little break," shifting to a whinier, drugged-out tone. "They told me I needed to take time off because it appeared that I'm cracking under the stress of being on top, but I know that's not it. They just want me off the air. They just want to replace me with someone new."

Amore seized the opportunity with his vulnerability. "What do you mean they want to replace you? You are him. They're not going to have another like you."

Rocking back and forth, "You're always expendable in this business," Dax snarled. "You know that as much as I do. You can be on top of the world for one minute, but you say something wrong, step out of line, or worse, people don't love you back, they want you out. You don't have any power without the people, but the people need to be blind to you and what you do. I am promoting new content. Maybe you can help me with that."

"Sure, certainly," Amore replied. "But I'm sure there are some rumblings in certain social circles that may have their doubts. Like you said, image is everything in this world today." In rage, Dax stood up so abruptly. "How so?" he shouted, sharp and raw. His body leaned forward, his fists clenched at his sides, almost like a dog marking his territory, daring anyone to challenge his claim.

"I've been the main guy for years," he yelled, shoulders tense, sweat glimmering on his forehead under the lights. "Whatever topic, agenda, story needed to be pushed, I pushed it. There is no other person than me. Rumblings? They can say whatever they want to say, but they will never have the balls to say it to my face." His voice cracked between pride and fury, echoing louder than the music outside the room.

"What do you mean there's rumbles?" Amore, feeling as if he could not move, he remained seated, steadying his breath. Rising to meet Dax's energy would not help here. He knew he had to let Dax burn off his anger before speaking. So, softening his tone, he played into the moment with a sympathetic calm that undercut the rage.

"From what I've heard," Amore said carefully, eyes meeting Dax's with a firm steadiness, "your name was mentioned with the dead girl a few weeks ago. Maybe they view that as a liability — something that may come back and hurt them, or hinder your ratings."

Dax's eyes scrunched, slowly returning to his seat. "What are you talking about, a dead girl? I just knew her." Remorse in his words, his emotions changing on a dime. You could hear the sadness in his voice.

"That's not what I heard," Amore insisted, poking the beast. "I heard you were dating her and that you were in the room when she died." Dax's eyes tensed up as he looked back at Amore. "Who told you that?" Downplaying the question, Amore said, "You know, you hear things." His heart started to beat more heavily. It could be the fear of getting this close, but it felt as though he couldn't really move. Thoughts within his mind told him to push through it.

It's just your nerves…

But why do I seem to fear talking to this man? He's in more control than I am, even in the state of mind he's in.

Seeing the tension, Amore changed tactics, diverting the attention. "How are your ratings? They're still through the roof. You still have popularity, and the guy that's filling in now doesn't even hold a candle with you. Even now your ratings have dipped since he took over. Maybe you need to focus on your team. Without a good team around you, you have nothing. Don't you have PR and handlers?"

Dax looked up, his drunkenness causing his eyes to tear up. "I did have a handler. Her name was Lisa, but she got in over her head."

"What do you mean?" Amore asked.

"She talked too much. Felt she was having a problem with me, with what she was told to do. She asked too many questions, and unfortunately, when you ask questions, you have to pay your penalty." A river of tears began to fall from his face, then without warning, an abrupt change of mood. A mix of anger and sadness was on full display. Launching at Amore, he grabbed him by his shoulders and looked directly into his face. In a hysterical trance, he said, "It's hard to find someone in this business who you like, and Lisa made me feel love." Releasing his grip, Amore could feel Dax's strength in his arms from the mark that had been left. The strange feeling of his hurt shoulder felt numb, as if part of his side was paralyzed. The heat in the room felt more intense. He began to cough, requesting more water, not wanting to stop the conversation. Lightheaded, Amore finally heard the words he longed to hear. He had confirmation that she was killed.

"So what happened?" Amore asked, his muscles tense with a rush of adrenaline. He was so close to cracking this case.

Now, more frantic than ever, Dax paced around the room, his steps uneven, hands shaking as if the weight of his own confession was eating him alive. Amore could only watch as things began to unravel for Dax. He appeared to be spiraling into a tirade fueled by the drugs, but disturbingly, he was still in control of his words, his madness sharpened into clarity.

"I told her, I told her that she needed to just play her part," he muttered, voice cracking with rage, "but she acted as if she was developing a conscience. We all have jobs to do, but it's unfortunate… because what happened next was that her drink was laced with something. Yeah, we made it seem as if it was a suicide attempt, but in reality…" He stopped, eyes dark, sweat dripping from his forehead as he clenched his fists. "…I had to hold her down while the drug set in. It wasn't something I wanted to do—but I had no choice."

The words hit Amore like a sledgehammer. In that moment, the weight of everything he had been chasing, all the lies, all the whispers, came crashing down on him. Yet even as clarity struck, he realized something far worse—he could not move. His body felt heavy, paralyzed, trapped in the chair as if invisible hands pinned him in place. His shoulder throbbed in pain.

Fear set in like ice in his veins. His vision blurred at the edges, sounds muffling into echoes as the heat in the room closed around him. His mind screamed, *"My God, what is happening to me?"* but his lips wouldn't form the words.

As Dax continued to talk, Amore's body began to feel loose, and his vision started to blur. The words in the room began to blend together, and then Dax dropped the final bombshell: "It's the same thing that was slipped in your drink, Amore."

Those words rang deep within his ears. Though he was under the influence of drugs, he knew he was in peril. He could not move. He could not breathe. His legs were heavy, unresponsive. Forcing himself to move, he attempted to get up, a final act of will to get out of there, but he passed out, falling into the darkness. His last thought was: He did not wish to die here.

Chapter 25

The Unfiltered Truth

White. White. White. Blurs of white began to form in his sight as his eyes slowly came back into focus. Everything around him was white — the walls, the floor, even the air seemed to glow. His body, too, was white, except for his hands and feet. Was he truly dead? Was he floating on a cloud? Could he be so grateful to experience heaven?

He closed his eyes again, exhaling as if surrendering to peace… only to reopen them and see the same thing — the same endless, blinding white.

He blinked again, harder this time. The light around him wavered. This cannot be heaven, but something else. Amore's eyes fluttered open with a cottony, heavy haze, attempting to clarify anything. With each moment, his eyes slowly began to perceive the blinding light. It soon took form in fluorescent light bulbs. He realized this world was a uniform canvas of white: white walls, a white floor, and a chilly, sterile ceiling all around him. No shadows, no corners, no shapes visible to give an idea of perspective.

Twisting his finger to give life to his weakened body, the first sensation was a numb pain, a phantom weight, settling deep into his bones. Each fiber of his body felt dreadfully heavy, as if each limb weighed a thousand pounds. He tried to sit up, but his muscles screamed in pain, and he fell back down. He was a puppet whose strings had been cut.

"Good," the voice said calmly. "You're awake."

A voice, calm and heavy with authority, came from the silence. "I wouldn't do that if I were you. You don't have full use of your body right now." The voice was unemotional. Amore snarled, his own a rasping echo. "Who are you? What have you done to me?" The words hung in the air, unspoken. He was alone, but yet he knew he wasn't.

As his body regained its strength, he reached for his chest, but couldn't feel the texture of his shirt — because there wasn't one. His body was covered in something thin: a disposable white shirt and pants.

With each moment, it was as if he was a child relearning the basic necessities of human function. He learned how to crawl, to walk, to use his body again. This was both a blessing and a curse, because now he was given the means to mundane life tethered by unseen hands, controlled by those who controlled him.

Days blended into a nightmare of repetitive routine. Footsteps. Slow. Rhythmic. Getting closer. White-robed individuals would enter the room unexpectedly, taking his vitals but never speaking a word. They would give him a white substance in a white glass, and he would shout questions as to who they were.

"What the hell…" he yelled, the sound barely escaping his throat.

"That's not something you need to know. You'll know soon enough," would be a cold, robotic response.

His own mind became a battleground, where daily sounds would pump in the room. The sobbing of an infant and the whispered words, "You killed me!" would merge into a single, monstrous entity. The sounds could come at any moment when least expected: during a feeding session, which the guards would witness unmoved and continue as if nothing were happening, or in the middle of sleep, to be kept up for hours on end. Amore's hold on reality began to unravel, but in his darkest moments, a flicker of defiance would ignite. He had to keep fighting; he had to hold on to the last shreds of himself.

Then, lost in the unknowing of time, the ritual was broken. A whine of the lights grew louder as a door on the far end of the room hissed open, revealing a figure in a long coat — face obscured by the glare. There was a grinding sound, slow and low, from the distant wall, and out of the blinding light there spread a vertical beam of light, stretching into a doorway. A figure emerged from the light, his form long and distorted by the glare. As his eyes adjusted, the form began to take shape. It was not just any man; it was Lucius.

The sight was so impossible to ignore, so unexpected, that Amore's mind wanted to lie to himself. "This can't be real, this is not Lucius," but it was truly him. It was as though reality had turned inward, snapping under the weight of the revelation. A wave of angry denial swept over him.

Fury erupted in him, burning away any signs of fatigue that had gripped him for days, weeks—however long this torment had lasted. Even in his weakened state, the urge to kill him overpowering anything his body could not do, he launched forward, his body fueled by rage. There was no plan, no thought, just a desperate, instinctive need to act—to tear down the lie that stood before him.

Suddenly he was hit from behind the moment he moved. Two guards materialized from out of nowhere, as if conjured by the moment itself, slamming into him, back down to the ground with unrelenting force. They pinned him down with terrifying precision, twisting his arms against his back. His knees cracked against the cold, unforgiving floor, and then his chest followed, forced down under the iron weight of their armored grips.

He struggled, teeth clenched and eyes wide with betrayal. Blood dripped from the side of his head.

"You!" he bellowed, his voice thick with a fresh convulsion of betrayal. Spit flew from his lips; his face contorted in rage. "How dare you betray me? You were supposed to help me! You approached me with the thought of a common enemy!"

His voice echoed through the chamber as silence fell like an eternity. Lucius stood in place, unmoving in the light, expression unreadable, the once-trusted face now a mask of terrible familiarity.

He refused to believe it. This had to be another one of their psychological games. "No! This cannot be! This is a cruel joke, a cruel game!

You're only a decoy, someone in disguise to look like him! I've been here long enough, this is the way they want to break me!"

Lucius's face remained heavy with a sorrow Amore couldn't comprehend, his eyes welling up with a sadness that seemed misplaced. "No," he spoke, his words a soft, somber murmur. "You're not hallucinating. I am actually here." He stepped fully into the room, and the door slid shut behind him, plunging them back into the soft, white light. "It is a shame it had to go like this," he continued, his gaze unwavering. "I am here to give you what you have been hungering for since this entire journey began—the unfiltered truth about what has occurred, and what is to come."

Lucius's words were a terrifying confirmation that this was not some fantasy. Two guards dressed in all-white attire entered, grabbed him by the hair, and restrained him until he lost consciousness. Upon awakening, he found himself in a wooden hut with the blinding whiteness substituted with the earthy, rich hue of wood. A banquet of his favorite food lay before him on a table. He ate ravenously, like a starving animal, the flavors a shocking contrast to the tasteless white liquid he was fed to consume.

Lucius's voice, echoing off the walls, shattered the moment of bliss. "Good. Finish quickly. Build up your strength, for this may be your last true meal."

Amore, furious, flung the plate against the wall. "If you are going to treat me like an animal, at least face me like a man!" But his fury was a small, fragile thing in this place where he could enforce no demands. Being placed in this scenery was no different than the white room he had been shackled to. The only difference is that they gave different contrasts of color, but with the same results — countless hours or days of torturous cycles, both physical and emotional. Stimulation of getting treated, then fed, to being starved for what seemed like an eternity. Sometimes they forced his body past its limits, shocking his nerves until his hands trembled uncontrollably. Other times, they played recordings of familiar voices — Naima, Melanie, even Greg — twisted and distorted, whispering words of betrayal and blame. The only act of defiance came with the destruction of the cottage. This was his only sanctuary where he felt comfort, but even in this, he had nothing. The realization started to form in his head — no matter what, he would die here or continue living in this hell. There was no in-between, no better remedy, only the harsh reality of where he was. He finally surrendered, a tired whisper of compliance.

Lucius finally entered the room. Amore's defiance was gone, replaced by a hollow exhaustion. Amore glared at Lucius, his rage still simmering beneath. Lucius simply gestured to a blank wall. Within moments, the lights went dark, and light began to project across the space. Colors and shapes started to form, revealing what appeared to be a news broadcast. The reporter stood in an area that closely resembled a place he had visited earlier — eerily familiar. As she continued, the reporter began to present the story.

"The man known as Stephen Marks, data analyst, was found dead within his apartment. There is no indication at this time on how he died, but he had been pronounced dead for the past few days. Authorities have verified there were signs of a struggle, but no one has come forward to testify. The last person of interest seen exiting the building was a male named Amore Reyes. He has been missing for weeks, and now authorities are regarding him as a main person of interest in this ongoing investigation."

Stephen's photo, a still image of him, enlarged across the wall — his eyes fixed on Amore, as if the look were saying, *"How could you do this to me? You let me down."*

The reporter's voice was a gut punch.

Amore's face paled with guilt. The words rang through his head, each one a hammer blow of betrayal and astonishment. The images ran across the screen in a blur: a chalk outline, a broken door, a grainy freeze frame of him leaving Stephen's apartment building. Paranoia clawed at his throat. They'd been watching. The whole time. He had a fleeting, horrific memory of the night, the frantic conversation with Stephen, the frantic hunt for information. He couldn't remember noticing cameras. He couldn't remember being followed. And yet here it was, irrefutable proof, a carefully constructed narrative to frame him for something he didn't do.

The anger, once directed against Lucius's betrayal, now poisoned with a foul guilt. He had led Stephen to his death. His duty, his "noble cause," had killed a man.

"You bastards," Amore gasped, the words trembling with a raw fury. "You were watching me the whole time. You knew I was there, and you let it happen."

Lucius's expression was cold and detached. "Stephen uncovered something he didn't have any right to know. He was good at what he did, but his arrogance was what killed him. He wanted to be the best, to be the one with the story that would make him famous. He achieved it, and it cost him."

"So, you just sacrificed him. FUCK YOU?" Amore choked out, his voice rising in disbelief. "For your sick game? You killed him because he was arrogant?"

"This is not a game," Lucius answered, his tone icy. "This is a declaration. We knew that your impulses would drive you to find Stephen. It was not a matter of what was thrown your way; it was a matter of when you would find him. Your drive would always propel you to this. We knew you would see him, and we made the call from the beginning. So now, the outcome was always the same. You had a meeting with him about an illegal breach of information, which resulted in his death. The world would accept this, and there's nowhere you can go.

The sad reality of all this is that you actually killed him. You knew the risk. You knew what you were doing. You could've easily backed away, but you didn't. You might as well have held the knife or the gun. They say you had nothing to do with it, but it is your fault — and you know this is true.

Amore shouted, "Why am I here? Kill me now. What is the purpose of all of this?"

Lucius looked at him with an almost sadistic smile. "Now that is the question I've been waiting for you to ask. You are just like me — a mirror of what I once was before I saw the truth. I, too, pushed the boundaries until someone came to me with a choice… just as I'm standing before you now, offering you the same."

He began to circle Amore slowly, his voice low but heavy, like a sermon. "This world is built upon the decisions of those willing to shape it. The 'circumstances' you cling to are illusions. You've been driven by your ego — by your friends, your family, even your own selfish ideas and thoughts. You've ignored every sign telling you to stop. You are relentless. You will tear down walls and move mountains to reach your goals; and still find nothing waiting for you but emptiness."

Lucius's eyes glimmered like a predator's, his tone turning darker, almost hypnotic. "You think you're doing good, but you're only acting out your own moral compass; a compass forged by the very people you think you're fighting against. You're not different from them, Amore. You are just telling yourself you are the hero in your own story."

He leaned in close enough for Amore to feel his breath. "But there's power in you. Real power. I've been watching you for a long time. You could be more than just another pawn scurrying across the board. I'm not lying when I say there's greatness in you. That's why I'm offering you something… rare. A role. A place. A chance to stop being used and start using others. To become what they fear."

Lucius extended his hand slowly, palm up, as if offering communion. "Be my apprentice. As someone once offered to me. It won't be easy; I know for myself. You must burn down everything you are in order to become who you are meant to be. Give up everything; family, friends, your name and be reborn. Or…" His smile widened into something inhuman. "…refuse, cling to your so-called truth, and die here, forgotten, or walk back into the world branded insane. It's your choice, Amore. The door to power is open. All you must do is step through."

Amore's mind was a turmoil of guilt, betrayal, and horror. He was no longer just a victim; he was now a criminal, one within a system which he had vowed to dismantle. He had walked into their trap, and Stephen was dead. The sight of Stephen's corpse, cold and lifeless because of his "noble cause," was a pain he could not endure.

He had believed that he was doing the world a good turn, but all that he had succeeded in doing was to have an innocent man killed. And for what? To reveal a system so entrenched and powerful, it could orchestrate his entire life, even to the exact moment of a man's death. Paranoia was a new, bitter fear. They had been watching him, a silent spectator he had never known was there. Every late night in his office, every quiet conversation with a source, every fleeting doubt he had about his own sanity—they had seen it all.

His own fate was beside the point. Whether they murdered him now or sometime later, planting a story about his death that would be as twisted as the one they'd woven about Stephen, or whether he spent the rest of his life branded crazy, it hardly mattered. He was already marked by society's standards. And the irony of it all was a bitter poison: the very people who would assassinate his reputation, who would write the stories declaring him a murderer and a madman, were the same journalists he used to call his colleagues. It was a joke, a sick, cruel joke played out on the stage of his own life.

But all of that paled in comparison to the dread that filled him when he thought of Melanie. He remembered the last time he had seen her, that unbreakable confidence in her eyes. He had made a promise to her in his head, a promise that he now realized he was not able to keep. She had been right the whole time. Even if he had published his story, he would never have found peace, would have simply moved on to something else and left her forever chasing the next thing. He felt a full, gnawing pain in his heart. Her happiness was more important to him than anything. His own life, his own bruised pride, meant nothing next to her existence, her reputation, everything she had built. If he refused Lucius, he knew they would come for her. Could he be so self-absorbed as to condemn her for protecting his own foolish righteousness? Or would he do what he had always done—put his crusade before her?

And there was Naima. She had been the first to join him, a young reporter with an unshakable determination. She was full of promise, a burning, shining talent. He saw her now, and the thought was a searing knife to his conscience: he would be killing her, as well. He had led her down this path, and now her future and her good name would be lost alongside his. It was the same sort of unwitting murder that he'd done to Stephen, but this one was worse. He would be murdering two of the people he loved most all for a cause that was doomed. The guilt was tangible, a strangling sensation that left him gasping for air. He was a killer, and now he had to choose who to kill next; him or his love ones.

The decision weighed heavy, pressing against his chest like a stone. But he knew—it was the decision he had to make. Regardless, he would not be coming back. Not as Amore Reyes. That man would fade into the shadows of his own choice. This was the path he chose, and now he would have to live with it… or die becoming something else.